BLOOD
AND
ROSES

D - ✓

ALSO BY MARK DAWSON

IN THE SOHO NOIR SERIES

Gaslight

The Black Mile

The Imposter

IN THE JOHN MILTON SERIES

One Thousand Yards

The Cleaner

Saint Death

The Driver

Ghosts

The Sword of God

Salvation Row

IN THE BEATRIX ROSE SERIES

In Cold Blood

Blood Moon Rising

Blood and Roses

HONG KONG STORIES VOL. 1

White Devil

Nine Dragons

Dragon Head

STANDALONE NOVELS

The Art of Falling Apart

Subpoena Colada

MARK **DAWSON**

BLOOD AND ROSES

A Beatrix Rose Thriller

THOMAS & MERCER

Published by Thomas & Mercer, Seattle

www.apub.com

Amazon, the Amazon logo, and Thomas & Mercer are trademarks of Amazon.com, Inc., or its affiliates.

ISBN-13: 978-1503944398
ISBN-10: 1503944395

Cover design by Lisa Horton

Printed in the United States of America

To Mrs D, FD and SD

Chapter One

Connor English sat in the open doorway of Falcon One, his legs hanging outside the cabin. He was wearing night vision goggles, and the arid and desolate desert below was washed with a ghostly green, the scrubby trees and lonely hamlets passing beneath the hull as the chopper maintained a steady pace of a hundred knots. The pilot hugged the contours of the landscape, the chopper's altitude never rising above fifty feet, keeping it beneath the line of the hills.

The pilot came over the troop net. "Falcon One to Zero. We just crossed the border. Now entering Morocco. Morocco comms, no chatter."

"Zero to Falcon One," responded mission control on the ship off the coast. "Copy that. Green to proceed."

Everything was taking place as they had planned: they had evaded Moroccan radar coming in, and now they had a clear run to the target. English leaned forward a little, the hot wind tugging greedily at the desert scarf he wore around his neck, and looked aft. He had a good visual of the trailing helicopter, Falcon Two. It was a hundred yards to starboard, maintaining the same careful altitude, head down and tail up, racing though the night.

Both birds were painted black and carried no markings or running lights. The two Black Hawks had been modified at the Manage Risk shop at The Lodge so that their radar cross-section was minimised. Stealth panels, similar to those used on the B-2 Spirits, had been fitted. The rotors had been modified with decibel mufflers. There were engine shields, a retractable undercarriage and refuelling probe, rotor covers, an extra rotor blade and a totally redesigned and enclosed tail boom. The Navy had done something similar with the birds that had been used on the mission to take out bin Laden, but one of those had crashed. The Pakistanis had sold the wreckage to an anonymous subsidiary of Manage Risk for twenty million dollars. The R&D shop had reverse-engineered the modifications and perfected them. The cost was significant, more millions, but the company would eventually sell it back to the American government, and in the meantime, it was going to prove very useful.

Especially tonight.

The price of all the extra work was that they flew more slowly than a standard MH-60 and packed less punch, but they had excellent radar defeat, and stealth was the most important thing tonight. English had been with the rest of the team when the hangar had been opened to the North Carolina sunlight and the birds revealed. The R&D guy responsible for the program admitted that he had been tempted to kill it more than once and that although the birds had been tested, they had never been tested with a full combat load, and had certainly never been tested on something like this.

This illicit trip into Moroccan airspace was their maiden outing.

The men inside the Stealth Hawk bore no identification.

The two helos and their complement of men were anonymous.

Deniable.

Unsanctioned.

Criminal, even, when you came down to it.

If anything went wrong, if the birds crashed or got shot down, if they compromised the mission in any way, they would be on their own.

English scanned the hills and valleys, looking for landmarks that he might recognise. He had studied the satellite intel that they had bought from the CIA. That had been helpful, but not nearly as profitable as the week that he had spent in the city itself. They had picked Beatrix Rose up at Casablanca airport and followed her to Marrakech. English himself had followed on the next available flight out of Basra.

He had taken advantage of the week to acclimatise himself to the target and the surrounding neighbourhood. They had considered several ways of achieving the mission objective. They could have assaulted the riad from the ground, but it was buried deep within the medina with very poor access. Some of the alleyways that they would need to negotiate were barely wide enough for travel in single file, especially true for the big men in the chopper with their hefty packs. The alleys were potential choke points, and that made English nervous.

So he had proposed this alternative.

They would fly in and attack from above.

The initial plan had been to take the target out when she was outside the riad, but in the time that English had spent in the city he hadn't seen her once. She was holed up. That wasn't really a surprise. She had received the same training as he had and she would have known, without question, that what she had already done demanded a response.

Oliver Spenser.

Joshua Joyce.

Lydia Chisholm.

Bryan Duffy.

The four of them had been assassinated, and they hadn't managed to lay a glove on her.

She had a list, and there could only be another two names on it.

Control.

Him.

They had to strike first.

The roar of the chopper's twin General Electric T700 turboshaft engines filled English's ears. Little else was audible beyond that and the beating of the rotors. He leaned back in the cabin and pressed the wax plugs deeper into his ears. He could just make out the shape of the crew chief holding up five fingers.

Five minutes.

He looked back. Falcon Two flared and started to descend to the desert floor. There was an additional team aboard the chopper, which would serve as an emergency backup should they need it.

They had been aloft for eighty minutes already. The two Black Hawks had taken off from their Forward Operating Position on the Algerian side of the border. Their course took them northwest, just a short trip before they crossed into Moroccan airspace. Marrakech was two hundred miles from there. They had not cleared their passage with the Moroccan authorities, and if they were detected, they knew that fighters would be scrambled to intercept them. Being shot down was just one of many risks that they faced.

The cabin was dark, with a residual glow spilling back from the instrumentation in the cockpit. The bird had been stripped of its seats to save weight, and so the passengers were sitting on the floor, leaning against the side of the cabin, all of them silent. Four of the men had served as Navy SEALs from the Naval Special Warfare Development Group, or DEVGRU. Three had been Rangers, and the others were ex-SAS.

He glanced around. Each member of the team had years of experience, and each had a different way of dealing with the lead-up to a job. Some listened to music; others closed their eyes and visualised the operation. English was relaxed enough. They had prepared for the job, and every man knew what he was expected to do. They were all good, too. Manage Risk didn't employ second-rate operators, and these were excellent soldiers. The plan was sound. If they executed it as well as they had done in training, then everything would be fine.

The pilot of Falcon One came over the troop net again: "Two minutes. Stand by."

The men came alive. Those who were not already wearing their helmets and goggles settled them into place. Throat mics were positioned and radios checked. They reached around for their firearms and, barrels down, ensured that they were functioning properly. They were armed with an assortment of weapons: M4 rifles fitted with suppressors, MP-5s. Banner, the team's sniper, slid into the space next to English, with one leg hanging outside and the other braced against the doorway. He raised the barrel of his long rifle and squinted down through the optics.

The pilot's voice came through the fuzz of static: "Should be coming up just off our nose, eleven o'clock."

English turned back to the open door and the myriad lights outside. They had just passed over the fringes of the city.

The pitch of the turbines altered as the pilot powered down.

"Eyes on target. Stay tight."

The helicopter flared out and started to hover near the insertion point.

"See anything?" English shouted into Banner's ear.

Banner gazed through the scope. "Negative."

English stood up and heaved the fast-rope in its canvas bag to the open door. The free end had already been fastened to the mooring.

5

He leaned out of the open door, still thirty feet above the rooftops, and looked down: they were directly above the riad, the downdraft kicking up eddies of dust and whipping the laundry that had been strung out across a clothesline. Rugs hung out to dry were buffeted by dirt.

He matched the riad's layout against the satellite imagery and the video that the surveillance drones and satellite had shot last week. Everything was just as it should be. Moroccan riads were four-sided habitations, usually three or four storeys high and built around a central shaft that was open to the sky. This one was no different. Each of the rooms looked out onto the shaft, and a courtyard at the bottom was furnished with a plunge pool that helped to cool the hot air. There were trees and plants down there, too. The only way in from the street level was a thick wooden door that had been reinforced by iron bands. It would have been possible to breach it with detcord, but they would have the same problems with access. It wouldn't be a sure thing.

Banner shuffled ahead into the doorway, the rifle held in steady hands. His job was to cover the men as they fast-roped down.

English pulled the thick welder's gloves over his combat gloves.

"Falcon One to Zero," the pilot spoke into his mic. "We're in position. Confirm we are ready to proceed."

"You're green to go, Falcon One."

The pilot clicked across to the troop channel. "Green light. Go, go, go!"

English shoved the bag out the door, and the thick rope unspooled as it fell to the ground below. The other men were up now, crowding the doorway behind him. Banner was alongside, and another man called Mason was directly behind, gripping onto the nylon safety loop that was fitted to his body armour.

English felt a moment of peace. All the preparation, all the planning—it had all led to this point.

This was what he did.

It was what he had been born to do.

He felt his mind transition into a different kind of mode, a calm that was born of repetition and confidence. He had visualised the operation for days, and now it was just a question of putting it into practice.

Time to move.

Beatrix Rose found it difficult to sleep these days. The pain from the cancer in her bones was constant now, and she was loath to take the morphine that she needed to quieten it. She needed a lot of morphine now to do what a single tablet had used to do, and one of the side effects was to render her torpid and drowsy.

She couldn't afford that.

And so she was still awake at three in the morning, sitting in a chair in her large room. She had been reading a book, her eyes barely focussing on the words. She heard the helicopter as it approached. She knew, from long experience, that it was coming in low and fast.

Too low.

Too fast.

She pushed herself out of the chair, blinking back the sudden blare of pain, and limped across the room to the door. She opened it, moved to the balcony that gave out onto the central shaft.

"Mohammed!" she yelled. "Isabella!"

She looked up into the night.

The black helicopter slid into sight, flaring as the pilot fought the backwash rising up from the roof. It was a Black Hawk, but it had been adapted with baffles and panels that resembled the stealth fighters that the USAF flew. The side door in the fuselage was open, and she saw a flash of motion from the man holding himself steady in the space.

Shit.

Two long, thick ropes were thrown out of both side doors. They unspooled as they fell down into the riad. One of them fell all the way down the central shaft, the end slapping as it hit the floor of the courtyard below her.

"Mohammed!"

She forgot the pain as she darted back into the bedroom. She took the rubber tourniquet from the side table and quickly looped it around her arm, biting one end and pulling the other, tightening it. She took the syringe and punched the needle into a vein, depressing the plunger and injecting herself with the amphetamines that she had prepared. She removed the tourniquet and tossed it aside.

The rush was immediate and powerful. She felt tingling in her head, her fingers and her toes, and her heart beat a little faster.

She had an M14 chambered for .308 rounds propped against the wall. There were six full magazines next to it. The bandoliers with her throwing knives were hung over the hook that bore her dressing gown. She grabbed the rifle and the knives. She had a pair of night vision goggles, and she grabbed them, too, and went back outside.

———

Connor English held onto the fast-rope and kicked out and away from the fuselage of the chopper. The rope passed quickly through his gloved hands, heat building up in his palms as he slid down, descending rapidly through the aperture of the shaft and into the enclosed space beyond. He hit the floor of the courtyard and rolled away so that he was against the wall, covering himself from attack from at least two sides. He took his MP-5 and performed a snap reconnoitre of his surroundings: the shaft was twenty feet across, symmetrical, encircled by a balcony on each of its four sides; doors and windows visible behind the balustrades; no lights on in any of the windows; no sign of life.

The team had been split into two details of five. The men in Alpha Team rappelled to the bottom, and the men in Bravo started from the top. Alpha would clear up and Bravo would clear down until they met in the middle.

Beatrix Rose would be caught between them.

There would be nowhere for her to go.

English looked up. The chopper had inserted the top team and was pulling up. The plan was for it to move away from the insertion point, circle within easy reach and then return to collect the men when they were done. The plan allowed it to remain on station for five minutes. It would be too dangerous to stay longer than that. If they overran, they would exfiltrate through the city and rendezvous with Falcon Two on the outskirts.

He checked the courtyard. The other four members of Alpha Team were pressed against the walls, waiting his mark.

He raised his hand, ready to give the signal, when four powerful detonations boomed out from the roof, one right after the other.

He looked up.

White smoke obscured the moon.

A shower of tiny objects pattered off the walls and onto the tiles of the courtyard.

Ball bearings.

Shit.

Claymores.

He swore again.

A booby trap.

"Alpha to Bravo, come in."

No response.

How many of Bravo Team were left alive? Four Claymores. If it were him, he would have set them in the four corners of the roof, each with a sixty-degree arc, and set them to blow with motion detectors or acoustic sensors. The killing zone could be as wide as the whole damn roof.

"Alpha to Bravo, come in."

Nothing.

The voice of one of the other men in Alpha Team buzzed out of his earbud. "What do we do, sir?"

"Execute!"

———

Beatrix peeled out of the doorway and crouched low, finding cover behind the balustrade. The adrenaline and the amphetamines coursed through her veins, and for a moment, she forgot the pain and the debilitation of her illness.

She had to get through this.

She wasn't finished yet.

Her work wasn't done.

She could smell the explosive from the mines on the roof. They had not been easy to source, but for the right amount of cash, Abdullah had managed to find them. She had daisy-chained the mines together with detcord and linked them to an infrared motion-detection system, calibrated carefully to disregard the neighbourhood cats that gathered up there most nights.

But a soldier, fast-roping down to the roof?

Yes, he would be more than big enough.

That had been one hell of a big bang.

She had counted five soldiers lucky enough to have descended to the courtyard. The dark shadows had slid by her window, dressed in black and with night vision goggles fixed to their helmets. They were equipped with MP-5s and grenades. No insignia. No markings of any kind. That figured.

There was no profit in Manage Risk announcing themselves, but she knew that it was them.

She had seen Connor English skulking around in the medina.

She had allowed him to see her at the airport in Basra.

She had allowed them to follow her.

She wanted him to come.

She popped up above the stone parapet and brought the M14 to bear.

She saw a flash in her goggles and focussed on the open larder that they used to store their food. There was a silhouette there, limned in green, crouched in the doorway. The figure was in cover, and there was no shot, but Beatrix aimed above and behind the figure to where they kept the propane tank that supplied the range in the kitchen.

She wedged the stock into her shoulder, pressed her cheek against it and sighted quickly.

She pulled the trigger.

The barrage of six shots streaked out, each round slicing through the thin skin of the tank. The gas detonated in a huge bloom of orange fire that billowed up to the low ceiling and then blew outwards.

Beatrix's night vision flared sudden white and then settled back down, silver streaks crackling across the lens until they, too, had vanished.

The crouching figure was no longer to be seen.

English was buffeted by the sudden blast from the other side of the courtyard. He hurried to the entrance to the staircase and pressed himself inside. The shots had come from the second storey.

It had to be Rose.

He was sweating heavily.

It was all going to shit.

Already.

He had to assume there were only four of them left.

They were on her turf.

And she had been waiting for them.

Fuck fuck *fuck*.

Even if it was just her, alone, it was even odds now, at best.

Come on, he said to himself. *Keep it together. Do your job.*

He held his position and then swung around so that he had a decent view of the courtyard. The three men had checked the remaining rooms down here and indicated with closed fists that they were clear.

English nodded and pointed upwards to the first floor.

They skirted the outside of the shaft as they made their way to his position.

English saw the man in the robes a half second too late. He had been hiding in what looked like the dining room. They had missed him. He came out of the room with a Glock in his hand and plugged the operative nearest to him with three shots, all of them finding their mark. The man jerked and fell face down, tripping over an ornate glass table and toppling into the illuminated blue waters of the plunge pool.

English raised the MP-5 and fired on full automatic, sending a volley in the direction of the man in the robe. At least one round found its target and the man fell back into the dining room again. English put his hand to his grenade pouch and took out an M67 frag. He pulled the pin, counted to two, and tossed it into the open doorway. The grenade detonated with a muffled crump, the thick curtains billowing out.

———————

If Mohammed was still alive, Beatrix couldn't see him. She popped the top of the smoke canister and rolled it down the stairs, waiting until the thick, cloying, acrid cloud had started to gush out. The stairwell was unventilated, and the smoke would gather and sink. It would be impossible to see anything if they were coming up.

That would buy her a little time.

She cradled the M14 and sprinted around the balcony to Isabella's room.

The door was open.

Her daughter's bed was empty.

"Isabella," she hissed.

There was no reply.

"Isabella. It's me."

There came the awful *chack chack chack* of an automatic rifle, and the glass in the window went opaque and then crashed into the room. The rounds passed through the aperture, missing her by inches, and stitched a jagged pattern across the ceiling.

The shots were coming from below.

One of the men had stayed in the courtyard rather than come up.

She had been lazy.

Lazy and lucky.

She risked a quick look down and saw him, rifle aimed at her. She ducked as another burst of fire pulverised the rest of the glass. Sharp fragments showered onto her.

There came two crumps as second and third fragmentation grenades detonated.

The explosions came from the balcony that led to the stairwell. They were clearing and coming up.

She popped up and looked down again. Smoke was swirling out of the door from her grenade. The soldier had slipped into cover, but there was a large mirror fixed to the wall overlooking the plunge pool. She saw the reflection of the dead man's body in the glass, and beyond that, she saw the soldier who had shot at her pressed up against the wall directly below, otherwise out of sight. She fixed his position in her mind, readied herself and then, in a sudden dart, she plunged ahead, leaving the shelter of Isabella's room, reaching the balustrade and aiming the rifle over the edge and down.

She fired blind, emptying the magazine.

The moan of pain told her that at least one round had found its target.

Return fire from the stairwell missed her by fractions of inches. She darted back into cover.

She had a small remote control in her pocket. She took it out and held it in her palm, her index finger resting on the single button.

***

Connor English and the last surviving member of the team crept out from the foul-smelling cloud of white smoke and pressed themselves into cover. They had Beatrix's position now. English had seen her take out the soldier in the courtyard, and that had come at a price. He knew where she was, and he knew that she was trapped there.

She had an automatic rifle, though, and he only had the advantage of one extra shooter. It was close to being a stalemate. He would have to proceed very carefully.

He indicated to the other man that he wanted him to advance and then fired a quick covering burst to keep Beatrix in her hole. The man scurried to the corner of the balcony and crouched down behind the balustrade. He was fifteen feet from the entrance to the room where she was hiding. Close enough to roll a grenade right into the doorway.

English kept his rifle aimed steady as the man took two frags from his belt. He had pulled the pin on the first of them when the wall directly adjacent to him detonated in a sudden and shocking eruption. Fragments of stone and plaster blew out into the balcony in a lethal hail, and the compressive force collapsed the balustrade, sending jagged chunks of stone down into the courtyard. The soldier was killed outright, his brutalised and lifeless body tossed like a rag doll into the branches of the orange tree below. His grenade, blown aside, detonated five seconds after the blast from the mine.

English blinked hard until his night vision had cleared.

Another claymore, remotely detonated, hidden behind a false panel.

There was a thick Berber drape on the wall to his left. The force of the explosion had disturbed it, and as it flapped backwards, he saw a pair of feet in the alcove that was revealed behind it.

"Come out," he said.

Nothing. He stepped carefully over to the drape, moving away from the cover of the stairwell.

"Come out or I will shoot you."

He held his breath as the drape was moved aside, and a young girl emerged from behind it.

She was holding a Glock semi-automatic.

English aimed his MP-5 at her. "Okay," he said. "Put that down."

The girl kept the gun up. Her hand was shaking.

"You're not going to shoot me," he said calmly.

He took a step towards her.

"Stay where you are," she stammered.

He recognised her. She had been younger then, much younger. But then it had been nearly ten years ago that Control had sent them all to her mother's house to eliminate her. That had set in train a series of events that had threatened to kill them all. He took no pleasure in what had happened. It had been business, pure and simple. Beatrix would have done the same, had the shoe been on the other foot. English had children. Two of them. And she would shoot him in front of them if that was the only way it could be done.

"It's Isabella, isn't it? I remember you."

"Stay where you are."

"I'm going to count to three."

"I mean it."

"No, you don't. I'm going to count to three, and you're going to drop that gun."

He took another step towards her.

"One."

Her aim wavered again.

"Two."

Her arm began to fall.

"Good."

He took the gun from her and tossed it over the balcony, then reached out and grabbed her shoulder tightly with his left hand. He yanked hard, spinning her around and clutching her against his legs and chest.

He raised his voice: "Rose," he called out. "I've got your girl. No more tricks. Come out. No weapons. Let's get this over with."

He moved backwards to the stairwell, the girl in front of him as a shield.

"I've got no quarrel with her. She doesn't have to be hurt. There's no reason why she can't walk away from here."

He didn't see the blow to the back of the head that knocked him to his knees. He put a hand down to steady himself and turned around to see the man in the bloodied robe raising the stock of a rifle before he drove it, for a second time, into his skull.

Chapter Two

The riad was burning freely. The conflagration in the larder, where the propane tank had exploded, was the worst, but there were smaller fires on the roof, and the drapes in the stairwell had been ignited by the grenades. Thick clouds of smoke were uncoiling into the courtyard and rising inexorably into the night sky. She looked up, half expecting to see the Black Hawk framed there, but the chopper had not returned.

The rest of the building had been wrecked. There were bullet holes in the walls, one whole stretch of the balcony had been destroyed and she knew that the roof, with its beautiful views of the city and the mountains beyond, would have been totally obliterated. There were dead bodies strewn around. A couple of the soldiers were still alive, groaning as they came around, but they did not pose any sort of threat. Beatrix would normally have put them out of their misery, but there was no time for that today.

Mohammed had been shot in the shoulder and was bleeding freely. Beatrix took a combat dressing and applied it to the wound, trying to staunch the flow.

"We need to be away from here, Miss Beatrix," he said. "The police will be on their way."

"How's that feel?" she said.

He flexed his shoulder, wincing from the pain. "It is fine."

She looked at him. "You need to get away from here."

"No," he said firmly. "Not until I have helped you and Miss Isabella."

She indicated English. "I need to get him to the Jeep."

"It is in the usual place."

"Weapons?"

"Yes, and money and documents. Everything is there."

Beatrix turned to her daughter. "I need you to go to the garage and get the Jeep ready, Bella. Take the keys and get it started. Don't stop for anyone. Do you understand?"

"Yes," she said, quietly.

"What is it?"

"I'm sorry, Mummy. I should have shot him. I hid. They didn't see me. I could have . . . all the training . . . I thought . . . But I couldn't . . ."

"It doesn't matter," she said. "It's one thing to shoot a target. A person is different."

"I let you down."

She smiled at her daughter, trying to reassure her. "No, you didn't. You were very brave. And you mustn't worry, Bella. We're going to be fine. Take your Glock and hurry, alright? We need to move fast now."

Isabella retrieved the pistol from the tiled floor, collected the keys to the garage from the hooks in the lobby, opened the big wooden door and disappeared out into the narrow alleyway beyond.

English groaned and his leg spasmed. He was waking up.

The thought of dragging English's dead weight through the warren of alleyways to the garage reminded Beatrix how weak she felt. The spike from the amphetamines had receded now, and the numbing curtain of fatigue had started to settle over her once again.

Mohammed noticed her weakness.

"Come on," he said. "We will do it together."

They each draped an arm over their shoulders and half-carried, half-dragged English out of the riad and into the darkened alleyway. The riad was buried deep in the medina in the heart of the confusing nest of streets and alleys, and after just a minute, they had put enough turns behind them that even the sound of the growing fire could no longer be heard. Locals had been roused by the explosions and the gunfire, and they gaped at the two of them as they dragged English's limp body between them. Beatrix knew that the police would be on their way. It would take them a short while to locate the source of the fire, and that would, she hoped, be long enough for them to get off the street.

The garage was located in a line of similar garages in a side street that fed into a small market square. Isabella had raised the door and had driven the brand new Jeep Cherokee outside. The headlights were burning and the engine was still running. Beatrix opened the back door, and Mohammed grunted with pain as he muscled English inside. He pushed him across the seat and got in next to him, taking a semi-automatic from beneath his *djellaba* and aiming it across his lap into the man's ribs.

Beatrix went into the garage and dragged a large bug-out bag out from the wall so that she could open it and check the contents. There was an AR-15 with folding buttstock, a Glock .45mm and a serrated knife. There was a large amount of money and, in a plastic sleeve, two different passports for herself and Isabella. The credit card hidden in one of the passports accessed a blind account in the Cayman Islands. She winced in pain as she hoisted the straps up onto her shoulders and carried the bag to the Jeep.

She returned to the garage to close the door, fastening it with a padlock, even though she knew that she would never return.

Isabella had shuffled across to the passenger seat. Beatrix got in, put the Jeep into gear and drove away.

———⌣———

Connor English felt the bite of plastic cuffs as he came around properly. His hands were behind his back, between his body and the leather seat that he was sitting on. He pulled gently and felt the edge cutting against the soft flesh on the back of his wrists.

He remembered what had happened.

He opened his eyes a crack. They were on the outskirts of the city. He saw the road signs for Tahnaout and Asni and knew that they must be heading south, into the desert, most likely along the R203. He lay still for a moment, preferring that they think he was still unconscious so that he might better assess his situation.

He was in the back of a car. The man in the robe, the one who had been shot and wounded, was next to him. There was a semi-automatic in his lap, the muzzle pointed at him and the man's finger through the trigger guard. The girl, Isabella, was in the passenger seat. Beatrix was driving. It was quiet, no conversation. The only sound was the rumble of the tires as they traversed the uneven asphalt.

He would have been able to take out the man in the robe, even with his arms restrained, but not Beatrix Rose.

They drove on until the overhead street lamps that striped across the front and then the back windows of the Jeep became less frequent, and then, after thirty minutes, they did not come again. He opened his eyes a little and looked out the window.

The angle offered a restricted view. He could see the swaying tops of palm trees, but no buildings. They were out in the desert proper now.

The car slowed and bumped as they left the road for a rutted track. They drove for another five minutes until they slowed again and rolled to a halt.

"Stay in the car," Beatrix said to her daughter.

The girl did not argue.

The driver's side door opened and closed, and then the door next to English opened. Cool night air swirled inside. Hands grabbed him by the shoulders and dragged him out, dumping him face first in the dust.

"Get up," she said. "I know you're awake."

He managed to get his knees beneath him, worked his right foot around so that he could push and stagger upright.

They had driven off the road along the course of a *wadi*. The desiccated watercourse petered out just ahead, no longer passable for the Jeep, and the moonlight illuminated a seemingly unending landscape that stretched out beyond. Dunes rose and fell as far as he could see, an endless lunar landscape.

He turned. The Jeep's headlights were on, shining right into his eyes. Beatrix was silhouetted by them, but even as he squinted, he could see that she had a pistol aimed at his head. She flicked it in the direction of the dunes. He turned away, and she kicked him in the backside, propelling him onwards.

"Rose . . ." he started.

"Shut up."

"Please . . ."

"Shut up or I'll do it right here."

He was quiet. All he could hear was the sound of their feet crunching through the sand, and somewhere overhead a solitary eagle-owl called out.

They walked for five minutes, until all they could see of the headlights was a muted corona that glowed over the top of the dunes.

"Far enough."

He stopped.

"On your knees."

"Rose . . ."

She kicked him in the back of the knees, and he fell onto his face.

"You have anything you want to say to me?"

"You knew we were coming."

"Of course."

"We had to. What did you expect? After what you've already done, you didn't give us any choice."

"Probably not."

"When did you know?"

"I saw you in Basra. At the airport. You should've taken your shot then. Shouldn't have let me get back to my own territory. That was a bad mistake."

He shook his head. "You saw me there? Fuck."

"Don't take it personally. I've been looking over my shoulder for the better part of a decade. I don't miss much."

"And then in the city?"

"We saw you in the medina. We had cameras in the streets around the riad. My daughter's been following you, actually."

"I didn't see her."

"No, because she's very good, too, and you wouldn't have been looking for a child." Beatrix shifted her weight, the gun never wavering. "But that's all over now, isn't it? And after you, there's only one more left."

"He'll be very different."

"No, he won't."

"You've got no idea, Rose. You'll never get to him."

23

"I got to all the rest of you, didn't I? He won't be any different."

"No," he said. "He will. He knows you want him more than the rest of us. He's paranoid. You've put the fear of God into him. He won't put himself in a position where you can get to him."

"That might be relevant if I had anything to lose, but I don't."

"Of course you do. What about your girl?"

It was as if the mention of the girl triggered the prolonged and vicious cough that wracked her body for a long ten seconds. She bent double and retched, and when she was finished, she spat a mouthful of crimson blood onto the sand. She paused for a moment, as if gathering her strength.

English watched and waited. "Jesus. What's *wrong* with you?"

"I have cancer," she said.

"What?"

"Advanced. I don't have much time." She coughed again, although the red puddle congealing in the sand made added emphasis unnecessary. The cough changed into something else, and he realised, after a moment, that she was laughing. "It's funny," she said. "You only had to wait two more months, and I wouldn't have been a problem any more."

She coughed again. It was a wet, hacking sound.

"You want this on your conscience, then?"

She laughed. "Please."

He flexed his arms against the cuffs.

"It's the end of the line for you, Number Nine."

The cuffs were strong, and even if he could have broken free, she had a gun and he didn't. She might have been ill and weak, but she was still Number One, and he had seen, up close and in living colour, that she had lost very little of her terrible edge.

"Come on," he said. "I could help you."

She shook her head. "What could you offer me?"

"I could tell you where to find him."

"I could find that out anyway." She paused. "I'm not going to offer to spare you, because that is something I cannot do. But if you make your last few minutes on this Earth cooperative ones, I promise you I'll make it quick."

He sighed out a long breath. There was nothing he could do. Grim fatalism settled over him. He knew that there could be no negotiation, and knowing that, what was served by prolonging things? And besides, he didn't owe Control anything. You could even say that this whole mess was of the man's own making. They had all been in it together, and his genius had made them all rich, but if it wasn't for his genius and his avarice then they would not have been in that East London house on that afternoon a decade ago. Her husband would not have been killed, her daughter would not have been taken from her, and perhaps she would not have scythed through them all with the bright fire of her vengeance.

"Alright," he said. "I'll help you."

"Why?"

"Five of us are dead—or about to be dead. Why should *he* be any different? And maybe you've got a point. I don't dodge guilt, and I don't welsh out of paying my comeuppance. You have a legitimate reason for doing what you're doing. You deserve your revenge and we deserve to die."

"I'm listening."

"Manage Risk has a facility in North Carolina. We call it The Lodge. It's huge, enormous, out in the middle of the swamp. It's very heavily guarded. Lots of men, lots of equipment. Mines, motion sensors, cameras. I know you're good, but this would be a big deal even if you were at a hundred per cent, and obviously you're not. You'd never make it."

"So? What would you do?"

"Get him to come to you."

"And how would you do that?"

"He has children."

———

Beatrix shoved the pistol back into its holster and fixed the retention strap as she stalked back to the Jeep. She had been true to her word.

One shot to the back of the head.

She had left the body in the dirt. The desert foxes and the vultures would see that it disappeared.

He had been useful. She would have to confirm his information, of course, but there was no reasonable motive for him to lie.

If he was right, they had a trip to make.

North Carolina, eventually, but a layover first.

She had always intended to visit New York with Isabella before she died.

Now she would have her chance.

Chapter Three

There had been additional Manage Risk operatives aboard Falcon Two, the second modified Black Hawk that had participated in the botched operation. The chopper had landed in the desert, and four of the men it had carried had disembarked as soon as the signal had been received that the mission was a scratch. Falcon Two had waited just as long as it took Falcon One to return and refuel from the bowser that had rumbled in earlier, and then both birds had taken off again and headed back to Algeria.

The four men had not waited to see that. They had orders to follow and were already working their way back inside the city limits, arriving at the medina just as dawn was breaking.

They were damage limitation.

Rapid response.

Reinforcements.

Whatever was required.

The men had driven into the medina and then picked their way to the riad. They kept a close watch on the property all day. They had found a vantage point on the roof of an adjoining property, forcing their way into the building and shooting the owner when he suggested that they should leave. They had broiled in the sun all morning and afternoon, watching discreetly as the police had arrived to pore over the still-smoking remains of the roof, noting the blast damage in the corners that must have marked the location of the claymore mines that had taken out half of the assaulters.

The man arrived later. They recognised him from the mission briefing: grey-haired, wiry and obviously fit. An ex-soldier, they had read; years of service with the Moroccan army. He had evidently been wounded; he moved gingerly, favouring his left arm. The police spoke to him at length and the men were concerned that they might take him into custody for further questioning.

They did not.

That was good.

He was with a woman. She was questioned, too.

They waited until the police had left and then they had gone down into the alleyways that wound their way around the properties in this part of the city. They took up discreet positions at the ends of the alley that led to the riad, good viewing spots where they would have plenty of notice if they were approached.

One of them collected the large people carrier that they had used to drive into town and parked it close by.

They waited.

The man and the woman emerged from the riad just after dusk had cowled the flaming sun. They paused at the door, conferring, and then headed in the direction of the first two-man team.

The second team slipped out of hiding and followed, their palms resting around the butts of the semi-automatic pistols that were holstered beneath their jackets.

The men were special forces: one SAS, two Delta, one Mossad. They were all trained in snatching targets from the street. They were good, and they were careful.

28

Whatever had happened to the men in Falcon One that had caused the failure of the mission, it was not going to happen to them.

An unspoken signal was exchanged.

The woman was slightly behind the man. The operative to her right jammed his pistol into her ribs and pressed his hand around her mouth.

The man was ahead and did not notice what had happened to his wife. The first team waited until he was alongside and took him, grabbing his arms and impelling him into the street.

The car sped in reverse onto the road, the rear door already pushed all the way open.

The man was thrown across the back seat.

The woman was bundled inside.

The three men came next, the last man slamming the door shut behind him.

"Go," he barked out.

The driver took his foot off the brake and buried the gas pedal. The car leapt into the road.

There had been a handful of bystanders who had seen what had happened. They stood around, exchanging glances with confused expressions on their faces. It had all taken less then fifteen seconds.

That was as long as it took to make a man and a woman disappear.

Chapter Four

The man they called Control stood at the railings of the big superyacht and looked out at the northern coast of Morocco. The yacht was named the *Mary Jane* for the mother of the chairman of Manage Risk. She had cost north of a hundred million dollars when she had been acquired from a Russian oligarch who had fallen on difficult times. It was something of a vanity purchase for the company, but also a useful way to defray the tax owed after a particularly profitable year. She was employed for hospitality for the most part, but occasionally, like now, she served time as a luxury mobile command and control centre.

The yacht was a monster, three hundred feet long and equipped with a helipad, two swimming pools, a disco and a cinema. The bridge was encased behind armour-plated panels, bulletproof glass protected the windows and it had its own missile defence system. Everything was pristine. The deck was mopped clean twice a day, and the metalwork was polished to a high sheen. She was managed by forty crew, most with experience in the various navies of the world, some of them ex-special forces. Even the galley staff were military. The captain had skippered an aircraft carrier for the US Navy before Manage Risk had offered to double his salary.

The day had been blazing hot, and Control was dressed in white linen slacks and a loose shirt in order to try and keep cool.

A steward came up from the bar and approached. He was impeccably dressed in the ship's navy blue uniform, a pin with the crossed gladii emblem of Manage Risk fixed to his lapel, and he bore a tumbler on a silver salver.

"Your drink, sir," said the steward.

Control took the gin and tonic from the man and sipped it. It was Hendricks, his favourite. He looked out over the stretch of water to the lights of the city of Safi. They pinpricked the dusk along the edge of a wide crescent bay, the pilot lights of smaller ships darting back and forth closer to shore. The port had a refinery and a terminal for coal and phosphate, and there was evidence of building works as they expanded the facility.

"Is there anything else, sir?" the steward said.

"No," Control replied. "Thank you."

Control saw the lights of the helicopter first, separating out of the glow of the city and arrowing over the sea approaching them. It was a Eurocopter EC155, a long-range passenger transport that operated off the back of the yacht. It had collected him from the airport earlier, and then, an hour ago, he had watched it fly out again, bound for a quiet patch of land off route R206 to the west of Ben Guerir, just northwest of Marrakech. It had touched down for just long enough to take aboard the six new passengers, before taking to the air again and returning to the yacht.

It had previously been quiet; the only sound had been the lapping of the waves against the hull and the clink of the ice cubes in his glass. The clatter of the helicopter's blades disturbed the peace and heralded the beginning of a task that he did not particularly relish.

31

Control watched as the helicopter drew nearer and the pilot, an ex-RAF man, expertly brought it down onto the helipad. The engines cycled down, and the rotors gradually came to a stop.

No, he thought, he did not relish it, but some things were necessary. He could have had someone else do his dirty work, but they wouldn't do it as well as him. Expedience demanded that he do it himself.

He was playing in a high-stakes game and he was not a man for cutting corners.

The door of the helicopter slid back, and the snatch team stepped out. The last pair brought the man and woman with them. Their hands were cuffed, and both wore black fabric bags over their heads. They were hustled off the helipad and down a flight of stairs that led below deck.

He finished his drink, left the glass on the balustrade and went down below.

———

They had taken the man and woman down to a large, empty storeroom two floors below deck. This floor did not enjoy the luxury of the floors above it. It housed the galley, the staff mess and the engine room, among other things. This particular room was used as a brig when occasions like this demanded it. The walls were bare, the floor made of varnished wood, and the only furniture was the pair of simple metal chairs in which the man and woman were seated and another, empty, that had been left for Control.

There were two men standing behind the man and the woman. Control nodded and they removed the bags.

He studied the two of them. They were Beatrix's associates in Marrakech. The man's name was Mohammed Elbaz. He was in his sixties, with a full head of grey hair, shot through with white, that he wore swept back. His beard was silver, there were deep lines in his cracked skin and his eyes were a soft, deep, chocolate brown. The woman was his wife, Fatima Elbaz, and was of a similar age, a little plump, and she held a pair of broken spectacles between her fingers. She raised her cuffed hands and slipped the frame around her head, pushing the arms behind her ears. The man's eyes were cool and assessing, flicking back and forth. Her eyes were full of fire and hate.

Control stepped up to them. He stood before the man.

"Do you know who I am, Mr Elbaz?"

"I do not."

"You can call me Control, and as far as you are concerned, I am the worst piece of news that you ever had. I am the man that the murdering bitch you've been sheltering wants to kill. I'm sure she must have mentioned me?"

"I don't know what you are talking about. Who did I shelter?"

He pulled up the spare chair and sat down next to him. "We're going to have a little question-and-answer session. I'm going to ask the questions, and you are going to answer them. I'm sure you've worked this out for yourself, but it is in your own best interest to make the answers authentic."

"I do not know how I can help you."

"I understand you were a military man, Mohammed."

He raised his chin. "I was."

"As was I. So you'll understand what it means to be obedient. To have the good sense to answer the questions of your superiors, and to be aware of the need for discipline when there is disobedience. Feigning ignorance is the same as disobedience as far as I am concerned. I would not recommend it."

He took out the packet of Marlboro Reds that he had bought at the airport. He opened the top, tore off the foil, thumbed one out and offered it to Mohammed.

"No."

Control shrugged, put the cigarette between his lips and lit it. "Your friend has gone to war with me, Mohammed, but that's not something that you need to do, too. I implore you not to do that. It would be very unwise."

"I do not know who you are talking about."

"There are ways of making people talk. I'm sure you know plenty. I am a student of military history. You must know, for example, that Moroccan auxiliaries committed thousands of rapes in the south of Italy during the Second World War. They used it as a means of ensuring the compliance of the locals. What I'm trying to say is that we all do things we would rather not do when it is in the service of a higher goal. And what I am trying to do with your friend most certainly qualifies as a higher goal." He very slowly, very deliberately rolled up the right sleeve of his shirt. "Now then," he said, as he rolled up the left sleeve, too. "Tell me. Where has she gone?"

"Who?"

Control nodded to the big man to his left. He came over to Mohammed and threw a stiff jab into his face, snapping his head so that the back of his crown crashed against the chair's headrest. He blinked at the sudden pain, water gathering in his eyes.

"I know, it hurts. But you need to keep in mind the fact that this is as friendly as this is going to be. My men have spoken with your neighbours, Mohammed. After the firework display your friend put on, the explosions and the noise, they were frightened. They were happy to tell us everything we needed to know. I know she lived there. Her, her daughter, you, your wife."

He glared up at him through the film of water in his eyes.

"Where is she?"

"I do not know."

"Are you sure about that, Mohammed? Are you absolutely sure?"

"Why would she tell me? I do not know. It does not matter what people like you do to me. I cannot tell you."

"I don't believe you, Mohammed, but I'll assume that she didn't tell you everything about her history with me. Allow me to give you the full picture. We used to work together. I was her commanding officer. She did things for me, and she was very good at doing them. Unfortunately for everyone, she put her nose in my business, and that is something that I cannot abide. I'm afraid I decided that the only way to protect myself and my family was to kill her. But I am embarrassed to say that what should have been a simple operation was botched, and she was able to escape. She had the good sense to keep out of my way for nearly ten years, but then, last year, she turned up again. Like a bad penny, you might say. Including the useless fool who failed to kill her at your riad, and who I must now assume is dead, she has eliminated five of my associates, and I know that I am her final target. So, bearing all that in mind, you'll understand why I am keen to find her before she finds me."

"I do not know anything of that."

Control took his pistol from his holster.

"My war was Ireland," he said as he ejected and checked the magazine. "Against the Provos. Vicious bastards, Mohammed. They had plenty of ways of disciplining those who they felt were out of line. Ways to keep their communities in order. They would beat you with baseball bats, hurley sticks or cudgels spiked with nails. But the one they liked best was the kneecapping. It wasn't just the pain of it, although that was bad enough. It wasn't just the incapacitation. It was a physical indication that the victim had earned their displeasure. It was a clear stamp of their authority, rather like prison, a visible sign of punishment." He shoved the magazine back into the chamber. "There were variations. There was the 'Padre Pio', where they put a bullet through each hand; the 'six pack', where they put a shot through each knee, ankle and thigh; and there was the 'fifty-fifty', a shot into the base of the spine with a coin flip as to whether you were paralysed or not. But it was the kneecapping that they preferred."

He took the gun. He smiled at Mohammed, but didn't aim it at him.

He took a step to the right and pressed it against Fatima's right knee.

"No!" Mohammed yelled.

"This really doesn't give me any pleasure," he said.

"No!"

He fired once, the bullet thudding into the woman's joint, wrecking it, pulverising flesh and cartilage and bone. She screamed, a shrill and primal noise that rang around the room.

"Bugger," Control said, looking down disdainfully at the splatter of blood that had leapt up onto the unrolled portion of his sleeve above his bicep. "Will you look at that." He took a handkerchief from his pocket and tried to dab it away, succeeding only in smearing it. "Disgusting."

Fatima moaned.

"Please," Mohammed begged.

"Again. Where is Beatrix?"

Mohammed looked up at him, his face twisted with anguish. "I swear I do not know."

He put the pistol to Fatima's other knee and, without further warning, pulled the trigger for a second time.

The pistol barked, the bullet thudded into Fatima's knee, she screamed out again.

"Please," Mohammed adjured, his voice high-pitched and reedy. "I swear I do not know. I swear it."

"Another question, then. We've noticed that she looks ill. Thinner than she was ten years ago. Looks like she's in pain. What's the matter with her?"

"She is ill."

"Cancer? The doctors we've asked think that's possible. Is that what it is?"

He mumbled something, too quiet to hear.

"Does she have cancer?"

"Yes," he murmured.

"How bad is it?"

"Very . . . bad."

"Terminal?"

"Yes."

"How long does she have?"

"Months. Weeks. I do not know."

"Who is her doctor, Mohammed?"

The man mumbled out a name and, at Control's prompting, an address.

"Very good, Mohammed. I feel as if we're finally getting somewhere."

"Please. That is all I know."

"I doubt that, Mohammed. Is she alone?"

"Alone," he said, forcing the word out through gritted teeth.

"Are you sure? You don't sound sure."

He whispered again, "Alone."

"What about her daughter? She was living here, too, wasn't she? Where is she now?"

"She sent her away. She has family in England. When she heard that you had left the country, she knew she would be safer there."

Control looked at him sceptically. That was feasible, he supposed. He knew that the girl had grandparents. Milton had ordered him to deliver her to them. It would be simple enough to check.

"You know something, Mohammed? I know you're deceitful. I know. And there are ways I could prove it. We could have you renditioned to someplace where we have the equipment we need. We could make you disappear, you and your wife, swallowed into a black hole where no one would ever hear from you again. But I don't need to do that. I've worked in intelligence for many years. And I've interrogated hundreds of men. You're strong, but I've broken men who are stronger than you. I've broken Irish Republicans who would rather have killed their own mothers than give me the information I wanted from them. And I became very good at telling when men are lying to me. I know when they are withholding information. You're good, but there are signs that you'd have to be a world-class liar to hide and you, Mohammed, are not a world-class liar. You know more than you've told me. I know you know more. You better start telling me before I start doing things to you and your wife that will make your last few moments on this Earth very fucking unpleasant indeed."

The man looked at his wife, and something passed between them. A shared decision?

When he looked back at Control, the fire in his eyes had rekindled.

"What?" Control asked.

"Could I have one of those smokes now?"

Control took the packet and offered it. Mohammed took a cigarette, slipped it between his lips and allowed Control to light it for him. He drew down, deep and long, angled his head a little and blew a long jet of smoke up to the ceiling.

He looked around, indicating the door to the boat. "You think you are safe here?" he said. "On this boat? You think this will protect you from Beatrix?"

"I feel pretty safe, Mohammed."

"Then why do you look so frightened?" He didn't take his eyes off him. "You wanted to know where she is. I don't know where she is now, but I know where she will be."

The two guards stopped what they were doing and looked at Mohammed.

"Is that right?" Control said.

Mohammed's eyes blazed. "I know it for certain. She will be wherever you are. Wherever you go, wherever you run to, wherever you try to hide, that is where she will be. She will find you, sir. And one day, perhaps as you wake up, she will be there. Standing at the foot of your bed with one of her knives."

Control glared back at him, knowing that the man was right. He *was* frightened. He was furious with himself for it.

"You know, Mohammed," he said, tightening his grip on the pistol. "I haven't had to kill anyone myself since 1989. I find it distasteful, if I'm honest. Much better to have someone else do it, but now, today, I'm going to make an exception."

He fired once, close range, and the man took the round in the forehead, right between the eyes. He turned to the woman. She spat at him, right in the face, the light in her eyes undimmed until he shot her, too.

Control wiped the saliva from his forehead.

"Throw them over the side," he said.

Chapter Five

Beatrix knew that this would be the last time she would visit London. She had checked them into a twin room at Claridge's, more expensive and ostentatious than she would normally have considered, but now, given the circumstances, it didn't seem so extravagant after all.

It had been worth it to see the look of childish delight on Isabella's face when she saw how plush her room was.

She had bounced up and down on the bed, and just for that brief moment, Beatrix had been able to see through the hardened carapace that the girl had created to shield herself from the unpleasantness of her upbringing. She saw through it to the innocent, youthful girl beneath. She was thirteen now, and older than her years, but her true nature was not very far beneath the surface. It warmed Beatrix's heart to see it.

They had ordered room service and ate it on Beatrix's bed as they watched trashy TV on the big LCD screen that rested on the bureau.

"So what do you want to do tomorrow?" Beatrix asked her when they had cleared their plates.

"I don't know . . . We could see the famous bits, maybe? Buckingham Palace. I've never seen it before."

"That sounds like fun."

"How long can we stay for?"

"Just a few days," she said and then, forestalling the girl's protests, "but we'll pack in as much as we can. And it's not as if we're going straight home, is it? New York is just as much fun."

"I suppose so," she said, brightening.

Beatrix looked at her watch. It was a little before eight. "I need to go and speak to someone downstairs," she said.

Isabella looked at her fearfully. "Who?"

"Don't worry. We're safe here. They don't know where we are. And it's a friend."

"Who?"

"Do you remember Mr Pope?"

"Yes," she said. "The one who came to visit."

"That's right. I need to see him, just for a little bit."

"What for?"

"I need to talk to him about what we're going to do next."

"Okay," the girl said.

"I need you to stay here," Beatrix said. "Is that alright?"

She said that it was.

⌣

Beatrix stepped out of the lift into the lobby. It was opulent, lavishly furnished, with no account of expense. She was dressed in sneakers, jeans and a white shirt, and she felt momentarily out of place. The feeling didn't last. She had stayed in places like this all across the world and had never paid attention to matters of status or class. She had seen many people die, plenty of them at her own hand, and experience had taught her that it didn't matter how much money or power you had. Those things were mere trappings, irrelevant in the end. She had killed Russian oligarchs, Taliban warlords and the lowliest conscripts. They all died the same way.

Michael Pope was waiting for her in the lobby.

"Hello, Pope."

"Jesus, Beatrix," he said. "You look terrible."

She smiled thinly. "I've felt better."

"Have you . . . ?"

"Have I seen the doctor? I think I'm past that, don't you?"

"But . . ."

"I can still do what needs to be done," she said. "When it's finished, I can stop. But not before. Stop looking at me like that. Do I look like I want pity?"

"No."

"So, you want a drink?"

"Sure," he said, leading the way into the bar.

He asked what she wanted. She told him to get a whisky, rocks, and crossed the room to one of the empty tables at the back. He meant well, she knew, but she had no interest in his pity. No energy for it, either. She had a limited fund, and if she was going to do what needed to be done, she would need to marshal it jealously.

She sat and watched as Pope ordered. He was tall and muscular, a soldier's build, but there was a sharp intelligence in his eyes that marked him out. Beatrix had fled from the Group by the time he had been selected from the SAS, but everything she had heard about him subsequently had been good. John Milton spoke highly of him, and that was a recommendation that she knew to take seriously.

"Here you go," he said, placing her drink on the table in front of her.

She took it.

"Cheers," he said.

She touched glasses with him and sipped the whisky.

"I hear Bryan Duffy's wife is making a lot of noise about what happened," he said.

"It doesn't matter."

"I didn't think you'd leave a loose end."

"She had nothing to do with any of it," she said. "And I'm not an animal."

"You know Manage Risk sent investigators out to look into it? I'm sure they got plenty out of her."

"It wouldn't have made any difference. You're a little out of date, Pope. Connor English saw me while I was exfiltrating. They came after me in Marrakech."

"Came after you? What does that mean?"

"A Black Hawk and ten men."

"A *Black Hawk?*"

"Yes, a fancy one. Quieter than usual. Didn't matter. I wanted them to find me. I let them trail me from Basra, and I was hoping they'd try and take me out. The place was rigged up for it. Made a bit of a mess, but it served its purpose."

"Jesus. They must be desperate."

"I would be, if I were them. There's only one left now."

"English was there?"

"Yes. But he's dead now. He was helpful before that, though."

"What did he say?"

"Everything I need to know."

"Like where you can find Control?"

She nodded.

"Where?"

"He's in America. The company has a place there."

"I know. We've had a couple of friendly faces working for us there for a while. I didn't know he was there, though."

"Lying low."

"Wouldn't you?"

Her lips twitched upwards a little.

They both sipped their drinks, a quiet moment.

"Did you want anything?" he asked.

"Just to say thanks. You've been helpful, and not just in Basra. I'm guessing you've gone further than you should have gone?"

Now he smiled. "A little."

"You didn't have to."

"I did," he said. "You sort of had me over a barrel, remember."

She smiled. "I know." She coughed, sudden and hard, and it took several moments to stop. "I'm alright," she said, waving away his concern.

He waited a moment, and then, slowly and carefully, as if unsure whether he was going to cause offence, he asked, "How long do you have left?"

"They told me a year, but that was a year ago. The chemo stopped working a couple of treatments back. I think it just makes the cancer angry now. There's no point trying it anymore."

"There's nothing they can do?"

"No," she said. "So it's probably not very long now. But it'll be long enough."

"What can I do to help?"

"One thing. If something goes wrong, if I can't do what I need to do, I'll need you to do one thing for me."

"What?"

"My daughter is thirteen years old. I want you to make sure that she disappears. Everything on her needs to be wiped. No birth certificate, no records of the time she spent in care, nothing in the Group's files—nothing. Once Control's gone, that ought to be the end of it. I'll be dead, too. But there are people I went after while I worked for him, people I killed, and some of those people have relatives with long memories. If anyone finds out that I had a daughter, she's going to be in danger. I want you to make sure that doesn't happen."

"That can be done. Where will she go? When . . . you know?"

"Better not to say. The fewer people who know, the better."

"Alright. I'll do what I can."

She finished her drink and stood to leave. The effort was painful, and she wasn't able to keep the flinch of discomfort from her face.

"Are you sure I can't . . ."

"I'm fine, Pope. Really. Making Isabella invisible when I'm gone is more than enough."

He got up, too.

"I'm serious," she said. "I appreciate what you've done for me. It would have been more difficult otherwise."

"You would've found another way."

"Maybe. But I might not have had time."

He extended his hand and she took it.

"I won't see you again, will I?"

"Goodbye, Pope."

"Goodbye, Beatrix. Good luck."

———

Isabella was asleep when Beatrix got back to the room. She went over to the bed and pressed the covers snugly around her and brushed the blonde hair away from her face. She sat on the edge of the bed for a minute or two, just watching the gentle rise and fall of her chest and listening to the quiet susurration of her breath. She thought of the last year, the time that they had been able to spend together. It was a gift that she had not expected to receive.

The cough came on her almost without warning. The first was deep, hacking and wet, as if there was fluid in her lungs that she couldn't clear. She got off the bed and hurried to the bathroom, not fast enough to beat the second wheezing fit that swept over her. She shut the door and turned on the shower to try and mask the sound, then bent double over the toilet and coughed again and again, harder and harder, until it felt like she was going to rip her lungs. Her mouth was full of warm fluid that tasted like copper pennies, and, eyes closed, she spat into the bowl.

When she dared open her eyes, she saw streamers of deep scarlet blood twisting and twirling against the bright white porcelain.

A curtain of darkness fell across the edge of her vision.

She gasped for breath, trying to stay one step ahead of the darkness, but it was coming over her faster than she could manage. She lost her grip on the edge of the bowl, her left hand stabbing down onto the cold tiles to hold her upright. The strength was sucked away and replaced by a swirling, seething well of dizziness. She fell into it, the blackness washing over her in a ceaseless tide.

Chapter Six

Control watched from the back of the armoured sedan as his driver, a former Navy SEAL, turned off the main road to Chesapeake and into the access road that delved deep into the expanse of the Great Dismal Swamp where Manage Risk had its facility. The company had purchased a vast tract of the swamp ten years earlier. The land was cheap because it could be used for very little, but it served the company's needs particularly well. It offered acres of land for training and battle proving, but more than that, it offered seclusion and security. The nature of the work that Manage Risk undertook made the company a prime target for the governments and terrorist organisations that would have cherished the chance to give it a bloody nose. The swamp, and the wide defensive cordon that it permitted, made it impossible to mount any sort of effective assault from land. Of course, some of their enemies had the wherewithal to make an attack from the air, but, as the sedan passed a battery of MIM-104 Patriot ground-to-air missiles, Control knew that they had that eventuality covered, too.

They called the facility The Lodge and the grounds around it The Site. The latter comprised several ranges, a half mile that had been furnished with cabins and buildings to simulate an urban environment, an artificial lake and two driving tracks. It was the largest privately held training facility in the world. As they drove through it this morning, Control looked out of the window of the car and watched as two big Grizzly APCs were put through their paces, ploughing through deep tracts of undrained swamp, throwing parabolas of spray and mud in their wake. Their big engines rumbled, loud enough to be audible in the back of the car.

As they drove closer to The Lodge, they passed through a twelve-foot-high electrified fence. The guards in the gatehouse watched vigilantly as they shouldered their M-16s. The car stopped, and the driver lowered his window.

One of the sentries approached.

"Morning."

The driver held out his credentials.

The man held a barcode scanner to the document, waited for the green light that signified that the credentials were legitimate and handed the papers back.

"Drive on," he said.

Control scrubbed his eyes. He was tired. He had transferred by helicopter from the *Mary Jane*, picking up one of the company's Gulfstreams at Marrakech and flying directly back to Philadelphia. He hadn't been able to sleep properly. Beatrix Rose was in his dreams, an avenging angel that would keep coming, relentless, until either she had finished him or she had fallen.

She had a list. There had been six names on it.

Five of those names could be erased.

One left.

His.

He closed his eyes and let his thoughts drift back. He thought of London, of his old office near the Thames, the position at the head of Group Fifteen that had seen him dispatch his agents across the world like his own personal angels of death. He remembered the *power*. It had been intoxicating.

One assignment was closer to the surface of his memory than all the others.

It was nearly ten years ago. He had been trapped, all of his options circumscribed until there was just one course open to him. He had sent five of his best agents to the small house in East London where Beatrix Rose lived. They had been given very clear, very specific orders. They were to eliminate her and any witnesses. But the assignment, unambiguous and simple as it was, had been hopelessly botched. Rose's husband had been killed in the mêlée, and she had been wounded, but not badly enough to stop her from plunging a letter opener into the throat of Number Five and shooting Number Ten in the knee. Only the abduction of her daughter had stopped her from attacking the other agents.

It had been a stalemate.

She had disappeared.

A decade had passed, and he had almost forgotten about her.

But things had changed.

John Milton had returned Isabella to her.

The shackles of the threat to the daughter that had restrained the mother had fallen away.

All of his old security became worthless.

And he had remembered her again.

The only impediment that had stopped her from coming after them all had been removed.

And Control had never been this frightened in his life.

They reached the first of the buildings that made up the facility, and the driver swept up to a stop.

"Here we are, sir."

"Thank you."

"Not a problem. I'll see you this evening."

———

Control walked into the main building and climbed the stairs to his large office. It was furnished minimally, with just a few pieces of furniture that each cost thousands of dollars: a glass-topped table, an ergonomic chair, a table with a sand-blasted glass top, leather armchairs. He stood at the picture window and looked out over the barren landscape, pockets of morning fog still floating over the boggy ground. He watched as another black sedan slowed to pass through the fence. There was another one half a mile down the road behind it. There was a board meeting this morning. The directors of the company were all inbound.

Every man on the management council had a gold-plated military, intelligence or government heritage. Jamie King, the founding director, was a former Navy SEAL. Reece Lines, one of the vice-chairmen, had been director of the CIA's counterterrorist centre. The other vice-chairman, Richmond Dodd, had been the government's coordinator for counterterrorism with the rank of ambassador-at-large. Other board members included the former head of the CIA's Near East Division, an ex-attorney general, a former White House counsel, a retired admiral and the former vice-presidential chief of staff.

"Morning."

He turned with a start. Jamie King was standing in the doorway.

"Shit, Jamie."

"Sorry. Did I make you jump?"

"I didn't hear you. Good morning."

Jamie King might have established the company, but it was Control's contacts and guidance that had developed it from an upstart collection of mercenaries into what it had become: the world's preeminent and most dangerous private army. He had been passing classified information to King for a decade. Once his role in the murder of Anastasia Ivanovna Semenko had been exposed by Milton and Rose, and he had known he had to flee the United Kingdom, King had offered him safe haven. He had been flown into the country under false papers and was smuggled into The Lodge. His role in the company could not be publicised, but he had spent the last year working with King to build it up even more. His contacts had helped to secure the oil contracts in Iraq, for example.

King sat down in one of the room's generous armchairs. He was, by nature, a serious man, but his expression was especially sombre this morning.

"What a fucking disaster," he said.

Control paced. "I know."

"What happened?"

"She had mines on the roof. It was one big kill zone, took out the second team just like that. The others got stuck at the bottom of the building. She took them out one by one. She knew we were coming."

"Those weren't Girl Scouts we sent in," King said.

"Doesn't matter who they were, Jamie. She killed them all. She's very good. I told you that."

"Yeah, you did. What about Connor English?"

Control stopped at the window and glanced outside again. "The housekeeper told me. They took him out into the desert and shot him."

King shook his head. "I've got to tell you, man. This bitch? She's something else. I've never seen anything like her before. Shame you two don't get along. I'd offer her a job tomorrow."

"And she'd cut your throat the day after that."

King laughed. Control didn't find it particularly funny.

"The housekeeper give you anything else?" King asked.

"He doesn't know where she is."

"You're sure?"

Control nodded. "He wasn't lying. He didn't know."

"Past tense? You got rid of him?"

Control nodded.

"Alright," King said, unfazed. "What *did* he know?"

"Connor English told her where I am."

"Big deal. She would have guessed that anyway. Anything else?"

Control nodded, reached down into the briefcase at his feet and took out a sheaf of papers. He tossed them across to King. "She has cancer."

He shuffled through the papers. "Really?"

Control sat down and exhaled. "He told me who her doctor is. We had someone pay his offices a visit last night, and he pulled her data. Stage four breast cancer."

"Terminal?"

"Yes," he said. "She's done for."

"How long does she have left?"

"Weeks, and that's if she's lucky. Could be days."

King leaned back in the chair and spread his arms wide. "So there you go. She's on borrowed time. You just need to wait her out."

"That cuts both ways, Jamie. The other way to look at it is that she has nothing to lose."

"What about her girl?"

"The housekeeper said she was with her grandparents. I've got two men going to check."

"Good. If we can get hold of her . . ."

"Yes. That would change things in my favour. But I'll believe she's there when I see it. Leaving her there would be a big risk, and Beatrix is not in the business of taking risks."

"And the housekeeper had no idea where she is?"

Control shook his head. "She's doing what she was trained to do. Drop out of sight. Pick your battles when you want them. *Where* you want them. We won't see her again until she's ready to make a move."

Beatrix was like a shark. You had a chance when she was on the surface; at least then you knew where she was. But when she submerged, slipped into the gloomy depths, the only warning of her presence was when she had already fastened her teeth around your leg.

And by then, it was already much too late.

His face must have given away his disconsolation.

"Cheer up," King said. "Look out the window. If we keep you here, how's she going to get to you? A swamp rat farts out there, and we hear it. There's no way she can get through. *No way*. This is what we're going to do. From now on, you stay on-site. We keep you here, locked up nice and tight."

"I can't stay here forever, Jamie."

"You won't have to. She either dies first or we get a fix on her. You told me yourself. She's worked all the way through the six of you, and you're the last one standing. She's not going to give up, is she?"

There were a host of uncertainties, but not that. That much was for sure. "Never," he said categorically. "Never ever."

"And that's to our advantage. If she wants you, she's going to have to come here. On our patch. We've spoken to immigration. She'll fly in to Philly, right? Border Control sees her, they bring her in. We've spoken with Homeland Security and the police department. Anyone matching her description in town, the same. She'll be spotted."

"And if she isn't?"

"If she isn't, assuming she makes it out here, she's going to get taken out by a mine or a sniper. We've got two thousand men on campus, buddy. And there's just one of her."

53

Two thousand to one.

Those sounded like favourable odds.

Control wasn't reassured.

He knew what Beatrix Rose was capable of.

Chapter Seven

They flew first class to New York. It wasn't extravagance this time, but practicality. Beatrix was finding it more and more difficult to sleep, and the prospect of ten hours in a non-reclining seat was more than she could bear. The ache in her bones was constant now, and the morphine had little effect, at least not at the doses that she was prepared to take. She could have upped the tablets, no doubt, but she wasn't prepared to go so far so that her edge was blunted. It wasn't beyond the realm of possibilities that Control might find her first, and, if he did, she would need her wits about her.

It was quiet and comfortable at the front of the plane, and they watched a movie together before the lights dimmed and the crew prepared the cabin for sleep. Beatrix helped Isabella to lower her seat, covered her with the blanket and then stroked her head until she was asleep.

She looked younger when she slept, as if all that premature maturity was just sloughed away. Beatrix thought of the training that she had made the girl endure for the last twelve months, and not for the first time, she regretted it.

Beatrix went back to her own seat and pressed the bell to call the steward.

"Yes, madam?"

"I'd like a whisky, please."

"Certainly."

"Actually, make it a double. Lots of ice."

The steward smiled compliantly and went away to the galley.

Beatrix stared out the window as the North Atlantic glittered in the moonlight far below. She caught her own reflection in the reinforced plastic. She had a livid bruise on her temple where she had fallen against the toilet bowl. Isabella had heard her coughing, and then she had heard the thump as she hit her head and fell. Beatrix hadn't locked the door, and so her daughter had seen her on the floor. She had helped her to get up and get into bed.

Beatrix couldn't remember flushing the toilet, but the bowl had been clear the next morning.

Everything was tidy.

She tried not to think about what that must mean.

She closed her eyes. The constant thrum of the engines was hypnotic, and she felt her breath start to deepen. She knew this would be the last time she flew. There was no returning from the journey she was on.

One way or another, this was it.

A one-way trip.

No coming back.

———

Beatrix remembered the atmosphere of the city. She had travelled the world, almost every major city in every continent, and she had never found anywhere else that had the same hum of electricity in the air. She felt it as she disembarked and then as they traversed the airport, passing through immigration on their fake passports, but the full effect was only evident as they stepped out onto the taxi rank. It was indefinable, a frisson, a buzz that permeated the air like pollution, the conflation of taxis and buses and trucks and jets, of angry cab drivers, of a million arguments and a million reconciliations, the sound that eight million people make when they are pressed into a space that is only fit to hold half that number. Beatrix remembered it, and despite the ache in her bones, she smiled and turned to Isabella. Her daughter was smiling, too, her eyes shining in wonder.

"Welcome to New York," Beatrix said.

They took a taxi to Manhattan. The lights of the city prickled and then multiplied, the skyscrapers stretching up into the night sky and their glow reaching up into its dark vault. The traffic was sparse at this hour, and they made good time. The cabbie was an Egyptian, garrulous for five minutes and then quiet as his attention was drawn to the commentary from the Yankees game on WFAN.

The St Regis was even more impressive than Claridge's. Beatrix had booked them into the Imperial Suite at a cost of four thousand dollars a night. They were accompanied up in the lift by a bellboy who made a show of opening the door and then standing aside to let them through. It was plush, with European chinoiserie and East Asian furnishings set against red tones with crystal accents. Mixed stylistic influences and an open floor plan lent a residential flow to the space, and deep window seats offered stunning views of Central Park, Fifth Avenue and 55th Street. The bathroom was fitted in Italian Carrara marble, with double sinks, a deep-soaking jetted tub and heated floors.

It was pure extravagance, completely unnecessary, and Beatrix didn't mind a bit.

Isabella was excited. She had hurried to one of the wide windows, her face lighting up. "Look at the view," she cooed.

"Like it?"

"I love it."

Beatrix sat down on the bed and sighed with relief for the chance to take the weight off her feet, even if it was just for a moment. She would have liked to throw off her clothes and soak in the bath for an hour, soothe her aches and wash away the sweat and grime of their journey, but she didn't have time. She would have liked to enjoy her daughter's happiness for the evening, but there was no time for that, either. She was tired, but not crushed, and she had an errand to run that wouldn't get any easier the longer she left it. Time was pressing. They couldn't plan on staying here for long, and she needed to collect all the things that she would need.

"I've got to go out," she said.

"Already? We just got here."

"The sooner I go, the sooner I'll be back."

"Where are you going?"

"I have some things I need to find. Stay here, Bella. You can call down for room service. Whatever you want. Watch TV, rent a movie. Just stay here, alright?"

"How long will you be?"

"Two hours," she said. She went to the girl and hugged her. "There's a spa downstairs. Why don't you go down and pamper yourself?"

Her daughter looked at her as if she were mad. "Not without you!"

"Well, alright. How about we do it together after breakfast tomorrow?"

"Can we look around the city?"

Could they afford to tarry? Probably. A morning wouldn't hurt. Maybe even a day. And she wanted to spend as much time with

Isabella as she could. The time was coming when that wouldn't be possible any longer.

Beatrix kissed her on the cheek, grabbed her jacket and keycard, and left the room.

Chapter Eight

It was a hot night. Beatrix remembered New York summers and the humidity that squeezed the city like a warm, damp fist, forcing locals to dash between the air-conditioned oases of apartments, cars, shops and restaurants. She remembered one night in particular, the end to a long pursuit across the length and breadth of the continental United States, chasing down a double agent who had performed a midnight flit from under the noses of the FBI and the CIA. The man had stolen nuclear secrets from British and French companies and was rumoured to be offering them to Tehran.

She had followed him to the Bronx. The pathologist suggested that he had overdosed on a speedball that had practically burst his heart. That, at least, was true, although the lack of evidence of any predilection for narcotics had been puzzling.

Beatrix walked north, leaving the park and picking up a cab on Lenox Avenue. The driver was a surly Italian with rosary beads looped around the rearview mirror.

"Where you want to go?"

"Hunts Point," she said.

The man angled the mirror so that he could look at her more clearly. "You want to go to Hunts Point?"

"That's right. Is that a problem?"

"You pay me first, it ain't no problem. Twenty bucks."

She took the money and passed it over the back of the seat to him.

"Hunts Point," he muttered under his breath as he put the car into gear and set off.

He followed Lenox Avenue, turned onto East 125th Street and crossed the Harlem River on the Willis Avenue Bridge. Beatrix closed her eyes and focused on the aches and pains, quantifying them, cataloguing, trying to gauge how quickly it was getting worse. She felt tired and washed out all the time now. Sometimes it hurt to close her fist around objects. She knew that it was getting to the point when she would be unable to defend herself if things took a turn for the worse.

She just needed to keep going for a little bit longer.

The driver took them along the Bruckner Expressway, exiting onto Longwood Avenue. She looked around. Hunts Point was one of New York's main red light districts. The cheap rents and open warehouses meant that it had attracted an arts scene since the last time Beatrix had passed through it, but it hadn't been gentrified yet. It was the proximity to the truckers at the terminal markets and the quiet, isolated streets that made it perfect for hookers and dealers to do their business.

"I don't go no further than this," the driver said, pulling over at the junction of Spofford Avenue and Edgewater Road. They were opposite the entrance to the New York City Terminal Produce Market and its large parking lot, filled with trucks. A railroad for goods and produce passed between the lot and the road.

The cab pulled away, and she walked south until she was on streets that she vaguely remembered. The atmosphere became more aggressive, a pervasive threat of violence just beneath the surface of things. Cars rolled by slowly, middle-aged men with nervous eyes glancing out at the women touting for trade. Other drivers were hidden behind tinted windows that muffled the heavy bass that leaked out into the street. Clutches of young black boys loitered outside the entrances to lock-ups and small warehouses, the bricks covered with colourful murals. The remains of stolen cars were abandoned outside chop shops. A white panel van advertised "Ca$h 4 Gold & Diamonds," its paintwork disfigured with gang tags. The trees were thin and weedy, as if breathing this polluted air was stunting their growth, slowly poisoning them. Hookers worked the corners, and junkies lolled in doorways, begging for change.

She walked on to Halleck Street.

She remembered an old bar, barely more than a shack. It had been a clearing house for assignations and merchandise, the kind of place where you could get information about whatever it was you needed. It wasn't there anymore. It wasn't a case of a simple change of use, or even that the business had been cleared out and the building left empty, as had happened with many of the other derelict shells that lined the street. There was simply no building there any more. The block had been razed to the ground by what must have been a large fire, the blackened timbers that remained the only evidence of what had been there before.

That was annoying.

She kept going.

A man was slouched against the wall of a garage advertised as "Vallejo Auto Repair."

She stopped before him. He was scrawny, covered in dirt, and he looked diseased.

"Whatchoo looking for, lady?" he slurred. "I got crack, smack, dope. Whatever your heart desires, I got it. I send you to the moon and back, and product's cheap too. I ain't kiddin'."

She crouched down and took a ten-dollar bill from her pocket.

"So? Whatchoo want?"

"Just information," she said.

He reached for the note, but she folded it back into her hand.

"Information first."

"What information?"

"I'm looking for something," she said. "I want you to tell me if I'm in the right place."

"Shoot."

"You know where I can get a piece?"

The man raised his chin and nodded in the direction of the bodega on the corner.

"Yeah, baby. That'll go. Whatever you want, you can get it in there. What you want? A nine? They got nines, no problem, whatever you want. Pacho's the dude you need. You tell him Sidney sent you, aight?"

He held out his hand, the fingers extended to show the dirty skin on his palm, and she lowered the note so he could snatch it.

She stepped around him, but he reached out and snagged the hem of her jeans.

"You *sure* I can't help you? You look like you could use a fix."

"Yeah," she said. "I'm sure."

She shook her leg away, breaking his weak grip, and went inside the bodega.

———

The bodega was stocked with tins of food and bottles of cheap wine and not much else in between. It was obvious that it was a front, and when Beatrix went up to the clerk and said she wanted to speak to Pacho, the man disappeared for only thirty seconds before returning, pointing to the door behind the counter that he had left ajar and telling her to go on through.

She did. The room beyond was big and noisy. Beatrix guessed that it was the same square footage as the bodega outside, and she would have been willing to bet that it made at least a thousand times the profit. There was a table and a lamp with an ornamental shade that was suspended on a long cord so that it hung down low right over it. A sawed-off shotgun rested on the table. There were three old ratty sofas and an old fashioned boom box that was playing a Jay-Z record. The paint was peeling off the walls, and the carpet, which looked like it might once have been beige, was the deep, almost black of blood that had been allowed to dry and stain. The sounds of the city outside came in through the open window, angry and close: car horns, gunshots and angry voices.

Beatrix assessed. There were a dozen people in the room: a big and mean-looking man behind the door, dressed in a velour tracksuit, his pendulous belly hanging over the top of his pants; a group of gang-bangers playing NBA on a PlayStation hooked up to a big LCD screen; two girls, maybe with the gang-bangers, smoking from a crack pipe on a sofa in the corner of the room. There were other girls, barely dressed, zoned out on crack so bad they looked like the living dead, dancing somnambulantly to the music, watching a gonzo porno on another screen. Finally, there was a thin white guy, unwashed dreads leaking out of a dirty bandana. He was wearing a LeBron jersey, a pair of loose slacks and nothing on his feet.

He was eating noodles from a takeout box. He looked up. "Well, looky here. Who's this, Trevor?"

"Clipper says she interested in buyin' some gear, boss," the big guy, Trevor, said.

"That right?" He raised a piece of sweet-and-sour pork from the takeout box with his chopsticks, put it into his mouth and denoted the flavour with an exaggerated smack of his lips. He switched his gaze onto her. "That right, sweetness? What you want, white girl?"

He was white himself, but you wouldn't have guessed to listen to him. His eyes wandered up and down her body, and she felt a moment of revulsion. She fought it back and said, "I want a gun."

The man lounged back against the sofa and pointed at her, mimicking a gun with his thumb and forefinger. "She needs a gun," he said to the big guy, suddenly laughing with uproarious gusto. "You hear that, big man? She said she needs a gun."

"Heard that, Pacho."

"Shit! You smoke enough hydro, and you end up thinkin' you hear things there ain't no way you could ever rightly have heard."

Beatrix looked at him more carefully. His skin was pocked with old acne scars, and there were tracks on his arms that said he was a user. He had two big, chunky gold rings on his fingers and a heavy gold chain around his neck. He was older than he looked, maybe forty-five playing at being twenty-five, and there was a cruel light that shone in his eyes that said he was mean and worthy of her caution. He was the top dog here.

She looked at him coolly. "Do you have one?"

He nodded down at the sawed-off shotgun on the table. "Sure, I got one."

"One that I could buy from you."

"Shit, *sure* I do. What you want, a little Saturday night special? Somethin' that'll fit in your purse, but still big enough to make a mess out of someone who gets fresh with you when you don't want them to get fresh—somethin' like that?"

"A nine millimetre. Not too big. A Kel-Tec PF-9 or a Taurus PT709. Something like that."

He stabbed the chopsticks back into the noodles and stood the box on the table. "Somethin' like that," he repeated with heavy sarcasm as he reached down into the pocket of his pants and pulled out a small pistol. He laid it on the table and spun it, the gun rotating until it came to a stop, the barrel pointing straight at her. Beatrix recognised the new Beretta 9mm Nano.

"That'll do," she said. "How much?"

"What you prepared to do for it, sweetness?"

"How much?"

He ignored that. "See, I like to think I'm a pretty good judge of a person's character. What you say, Trevor? Am I a good judge of character?"

"The best I ever seen."

"That's right, the best. And I took one look at you as you came in that door, and I'm thinkin' that girl, man, Pacho, *that* girl who used to be fine not so very long ago, now she's just all the way desperate. I mean, look at you, all emaciated and shit. You been on the rock too long, baby. It ain't a gun you here for, is it? You here because you heard that the produce I put on the market is primo, grade A, number one top shit. That's right, ain't it?" He grinned at her.

Beatrix felt her anger rising. She spoke coolly and calmly, but it was difficult. "I want the gun," she said. "That's all I want. Is it for sale or isn't it?"

He toyed with her some more. "What you want a piece for? Boyfriend been hittin' you around? You and me, we work somethin' out. I'll send Big Trevor over there to pay his sorry ass a visit. He won't be a problem no more, and I'll show you what a real man looks like."

"I'll give you five hundred dollars for it."

He went wide-eyed, theatrically over the top. "You carryin' that much cash into a place like this? A white girl like you, little like you are, all skinny and shit, all alone?"

She took out her money and, with no nerves, counted out five hundred-dollar bills. She dropped the notes on the table next to the gun and then peeled off another and dropped that, too. "For ammunition," she said.

"Shit, girl, you got stones!" Pacho laughed. "You see this bitch, Trevor? You see the stones on her?"

"I see it, boss."

Pacho looked up at her with a predatory gleam in his eyes. She looked back at him, daring him to look away first. He baulked, hiding it behind a laugh, and swept the gun across the table to her. He picked up the box of noodles, extracted the chopsticks and pointed with them to the empty chair opposite him. "Take a seat, baby," Pacho said. "Let me get you a drink."

"No thanks," she said.

"You don't want nothin' else?"

"Just the ammunition and then I'm gone."

He leaned back and laced his fingers in front of him. "Like I say," he drawled, "when it comes to reading people, there ain't no one I've ever met can hold a candle to me. So let me tell you something else I seen in you as soon as you come through the door. I seen hunger. The kind of hunger that tells me that this ain't your first dance with the devil, you know what I'm talkin' about? You ain't here for a gun, least not *just* for a gun. You had a taste of the good stuff before, right? And you be wonderin' right now whether you might like another taste."

The shame of it was this: he was right.

She thought about it, and the more she ran it through her mind, the more she realised it had always been about more than the gun. She could have found a piece anywhere. She could have contacted Pope and had the local quartermaster meet her with practically anything she wanted. Getting it like this was crazy, unnecessarily risky, and she would never normally have taken an unnecessary risk.

She had known that there would be drugs here.

Heroin.

Her appetite had waited quietly at the back of her thoughts, just detectable but always there, and it had brought her here under a false pretence. Now, after it had put her in front of the junkies and their paraphernalia and their little packets of oblivion, it told her, whispering into her ear over and over and over again, that here was the answer to all of her pain.

All she had to do was ask.

"You like this?" the man said, holding up one of the little baggies. He flicked a finger against it. "I see you do. You want some?"

She fought the urge to say yes.

"Primo-fucking-grade-A horse, baby. Uncut. Practically untouched by human hands since it left Afghanistan."

She looked at the bag and felt the old rush of weakness that she had never completely been able to ignore. The morphine she had been taking had sated her appetite, at least at the start, but recently all it had been doing was just whetting the edge of her weakness. She knew, looking at the little plastic baggie that Pacho was holding between his thumb and forefinger, that it was the solution. That, right there, was the answer to the pain and the sleeplessness and the fear that she looked upon every time she closed her eyes.

"What you say, sweetness?"

"How much for a hit?"

"*Gratis.* Compliments of the house."

Before she could say anything, he took a brass spoon and dropped a chunk of the fibrous heroin into it, taking a syringe and squirting in a little water. He took out a lighter and heated the bottom of the spoon. Beatrix watched it bubble and spit as it started to heat, and the hunger that she had kept locked up deep inside her crept back up to the surface, avid, ready. Pacho dropped a cotton wool ball into the mixture and then slid the needle into the middle of it, using it to filter half of the solution as he drew it up into the barrel.

He placed the spoon down carefully on the table and handed her the needle.

"Enjoy."

She took it. She had only injected occasionally, now and again, preferring to chase the dragon, but she knew that this would be more intense and her need was greater. This would work.

She held the syringe between her fingers, gently rolling it one way and then rolling it back the other.

"Come on then, baby. What you waiting for?"

No.

Isabella.

She had made a mistake. She had always known it. She just needed to bring herself to the edge to know that it was true. This was the coward's way out. The pain was bad, awfully bad, and she knew that she could find peace by pushing the needle into her vein and sliding down the plunger. That was the void, and it had served her well enough when she had sunk into the squalor of the Chungking Mansions, when she had nothing to live for and when the possibility of overdosing was a promise, not a threat.

But not now.

Isabella.

She did have something to live for now. There could only be a little time left, and every moment was precious. She couldn't squander a second of it in a stupor. The pain was her reminder that, despite everything, she was still alive.

She was alive.

She laid the syringe down and rolled it over to Pacho's side of the table.

"What?"

69

"I don't want it."

Pacho flicked the syringe back across the table at her.

"No," she said. "I don't want it."

"What you mean, girl? After I went to all that trouble?"

"I'm sorry."

He leered at her, a wide grin that exposed his discoloured teeth and then, as he parted his lips, the damp red tip of his tongue. "You fine, darlin'. You sure there ain't nothin' here you want?"

Beatrix closed her fists and hoped, prayed, that he wasn't going to do something stupid that would get him and everyone else in the room killed, but he spread his legs and nodded down at his crotch, and she knew that it was all about to get real.

"No," she said, scoping out the room with fresh eyes. "I'm sure. Thanks."

"Come on, don't be like that." He looked over at the big black guy at the door. "Trevor," he called out, "lock the door and get over here, aight? She don't think she want to partake of everything we got to offer, but I know she does."

"I've made a mistake," she said. "I'm sorry to disturb you. I need to be going."

He picked up the chopsticks again and stabbed another piece of meat. "Naw, you ain't made a mistake," he said as he deposited the pork in his mouth. "You pretty scrawny, all elbows and knees and shoulders and shit, but that's alright. I ain't fussy. Most of my girls are like that after they been on the pipe long enough. What you'd call a vocational hazard, you know what I'm talkin' about? You, though, there's somethin' about you that I can't quite put my finger on. Maybe it's that you got a little fight left in you. Don't worry, you won't for long."

She quickly identified possible weapons: the pool table with cues and heavy eight-ounce balls; a bottle of gin on the table; the shotgun; the unloaded pistol.

Pacho got up, his knee nudging the table. The syringe rolled off and fell to the stained carpet.

She assessed threats: most of the others in the room were too far gone to be much trouble; the big black guy was packing—she could see the butt of a semi-automatic at the side of his khakis; Pacho could just reach out and take the shotgun.

He came around the table and stood before her. He still had the chopsticks in his hand, and he made a play of putting them in his mouth, one after the other, and sucking the juices clean off them.

"I changed my mind. I ain't gonna sell you that gun. Truth is, that's my new piece. I haven't given it a road test yet—maybe I'll hang onto it for a while. Maybe I'll try it out tonight."

Trevor had worked his way around her, and now, with a suddenness that took her by surprise, he lunged at her and encircled her waist with one thick arm and her shoulders with the other. He was as strong as a bear. There was a whooping and hollering as the others stopped to watch the show.

"Now then, I got a nice room out back where I take new girls. To check them out, know what I mean? I was thinkin' you and me could get to know each other better. I can't have you come over here and leave without enjoyin' my hospitality."

Trevor hauled her into the room, Pacho coming after them.

She jammed her head backwards, hard, and felt the crunching impact with Trevor's nose. He loosened his grip, and Beatrix summoned up all the strength she had left to break free of him.

She stumbled out of his grasp, her balance suddenly off, and walked straight into Pacho's heavy right jab.

She staggered backwards, and Trevor wrapped his arms around her again.

"You know what?" Pacho spat at her. "Your pretty face is gonna turn awful goddamn ugly in thirty seconds if you don't settle down and do what the fuck I tell you to do."

"I'm going to kill you," she gasped out, but it was a bluff. She felt weak and helpless. The pain was everywhere: the pain in her face from where he had hit her to the steady drumbeat of pain that was a constant all the way around her body.

"No, you ain't. You alright, Trevor?"

"Think she done gone broke my nose, boss."

Trevor's right leg was pressed up against her right leg, and looking down quickly to make sure her aim was good, she raised her foot and stamped down, her heel scraping against the big man's shin. The pain would have been quick and sharp, and he loosened his hold on her again. This time, she worked herself away just enough to raise her arm and crash the point of her elbow into his face. He went down, squealing, his left hand still fastened around her shoulder, and he dragged her down with him.

She clambered to her feet, struggling away from the soft give of his belly until she was on her hands and knees.

Pacho kicked her in the ribs. It was hard enough to raise her from the floor, and she collapsed down again, the breath punched out of her lungs.

"What's the matter?" he yelled. "Can't breathe?" He pointed down to his crotch again. "What I'm packin' down there, bitch, you better get used to that."

"You're dead," she gasped.

He laughed as he dropped down onto his haunches so that he was close enough to knot his fist in her hair. "Let me tell you somethin' else. I've been aroun' the block a few times; you could probably guess that already, a successful entrepreneur like me in this particular kind of business. And you'd probably guess, if you were asked, that the chances were I'd killed my fair share of people who got in my way, didn't do what I told them to do or otherwise just went and flat out pissed me off. And you'd be right." He yanked her head up. "You fuckin' listenin' to me?"

She was drowning in a tide of dizziness. He had pulled her out of it just enough so that she was able to focus on coming the full way back.

He was still talking. "I killed my fair share, and I figure I'll kill plenty more before I'm halfway done. And here's the benefit of my experience: the first guy you kill, well, he's the hardest one of all. I don't care if you're a psychopath, you could be Adolf fuckin' Hitler, and the first one is gonna be the one that gives you nightmares until you get it all figured out inside your head. The second one ain't easy, but it sure is easier than number one, and by the time you get up to where I'm at, twenty, thirty—hell, when you get up to thirty it's like scratchin' an itch."

"Who would've thought it?" she said, her voice weak and rasping.

"Say what, sweet cheeks?"

"I said, who would've thought it, me and you having something like that in common."

"You a *killer?*" He laughed and turned to Trevor so that he took his eyes off her for a second.

And that's all it took.

She reached out for where the syringe had fallen to the floor, her fingers grabbing around it, holding her thumb over the plunger and then stabbing it down, hard against Pacho's naked foot. The needle punctured the skin and slid all the way in.

Beatrix depressed the plunger.

His eyes went wide, and then he hopped backwards, comically reaching down for the syringe that was still sticking out of his foot.

Beatrix swept her right hand out for one of Pacho's discarded chopsticks, gathered it up and held it in her fist with her thumb pressed over the thick end to make sure that it didn't slide out of her grip, and then pirouetted on her left foot, maintaining the momentum as she raised her fist and punched the thin end of the chopstick against Trevor's fat, bulbous neck.

The chopstick was made of plastic, and it didn't shatter. Instead, it perforated the big man's throat and slid inside for a full three inches, right until the side of her fist ran up against his neck.

She let go and turned again, looking for Pacho.

He had dropped to the floor, sitting down so that his back was pressed up against the wall. There was an unusual expression on his face: the hit from the heroin had already taken hold, and there was peace there, his muscles relaxed and his breathing coming in and out with a gently rhythmic ease; but behind that bliss was terror, his eyes wide and full of it.

She looked down at him. She could leave now, take the gun and go. He was in no fit state to follow, and even if he was, he wouldn't be able to find her.

But she couldn't do that.

Trevor was on his knees, pawing at the chopstick in his neck.

She checked the room next door. The music still pumped loudly, the TV still showed the same cheap porno. It was too loud, and they were too far gone for any of them to have noticed what had just gone down.

She crouched down at Pacho's level. "I didn't come here for trouble," she said. "I just wanted to make a purchase. A transaction, simple as that. You had to make it complicated, didn't you?"

Pacho's expression changed. It might have been a smile; it might have been what terror looked like on the face of someone who had just mainlined a jumbo hit of heroin.

He had managed to remove the syringe from his foot. Beatrix collected it and checked that it was intact. It was. There was a cord from a dressing gown on the chair, and she took it. She looped it around his arm, right above the elbow, and knotted it tight.

"I've done some things in my time, Pacho, things that would make your head spin. I was hoping that those days were almost behind me. But maybe they're not. Maybe they never will be." She took the syringe, held the needle in the liquid that remained in the spoon, and drew it up into the barrel. There was enough remaining in the spoon to fill the syringe again. "Because one thing I know, and I know it absolutely for sure, I can't live with the thought of a son of a bitch like you walking around breathing the same air as my daughter."

Beatrix took his arm again and pressed the needle into a plump, inviting vein. She pushed down on the plunger, watching the heroin slowly disappear, a thread of his scarlet blood appearing in the yellowish fluid until it was all gone. He sighed, tranquil and restful, and his eyes rolled up into his head as his lids slowly descended.

There was a bag in front of Pacho. She opened it and found two cling-filmed bricks of cocaine and ten thick bundles of dollar notes. She dumped the coke on the floor, collected the pistol from the table and dropped it into the bag.

Beatrix went back into the main room and grabbed the sawed-off from the table. "No one moves," she said, racking the slide. The double click, its promise horribly evocative, underlined the threat that she posed.

"Where's the ammunition?" she called out to the gang-bangers.

One of them hurried across the room to a cupboard, returning with a box of 9mm rounds for the pistol and a box of 12-gauge double-ought buckshot for the shotgun. Beatrix dropped the boxes in the bag, zipped it up and, covering herself with the sawed-off, backed across to the door. No one moved.

She went through into the bodega, covering the clerk with the gun.

"You got a car?" she said.

He stared at the gun, his eyes wide. "The Impala," he said. "Outside."

She waved the sawed-off in his face. "Keys."

He fumbled in his pocket and handed her a key ring with three keys on it.

"Don't do anything crazy."

She went outside. There was an Impala parked on the empty lot next to the bodega. She opened the door, slid the bag and then the shotgun inside, started the engine and put the car into drive. She pulled away and headed back to the glittering lights of Manhattan.

———

There was a 24-hour McDonald's along the way, and she stopped there, found her way into the restroom. It was squalid, with dirty paper and puddles of vomit and urine on the floor, dried residue gathered in the cracks between the tiles. There was a syringe in the sink and other evidence that suggested this place was used as a shooting gallery.

Her mind leapt back to the heroin in the spoon.

She closed her eyes and forced the image away.

She opened her eyes again and looked up into the mirror.

Pacho's punch had glanced off her nose and thumped into her eye socket. Her right eye was circled with a black contusion that was already shot through with livid purples. The ring he had been wearing must have scraped the bridge of her nose, a long graze that had filled with blood and crusted over. There were no hand towels in the dispenser, so she stepped into the fetid cubicle for the last handful of toilet paper, soaked it in tepid water and mopped away the blood. Her eye was fine, but there was nothing she could do to disguise the fact that the mark was there.

Isabella would worry.

Nothing she could do about that.

She rinsed her face, ran her wet hands through her hair. She looked old, tired and gaunt, her cheekbones even more prominent now. Her hair seemed thinner, her skin more papery than she could remember. She would never have bruised as easily as that before. She was being eaten up from the inside, and there was nothing she could do to slow it down. She was on the home stretch now.

She just hoped that she had time.

———————

She slid the keycard into the reader, waiting for the *chunk* as the door unlocked. She opened it carefully. She had hoped that Isabella might be asleep, but she wasn't. The television was tuned to a late night talk show and, as Beatrix passed the bathroom and reached the bedroom, she saw her daughter sitting on the bed, her back propped up with two pillows.

"Mummy!" she said, sliding to the floor.

"Hello, Bella."

Her face dropped. "What happened to your eye?"

"I had a disagreement with someone," she said.

"Are you . . ."

"I'm fine. Relax. It's just a black eye. It's nothing."

She dropped the black bag onto the bed and unzipped it.

She took out the sawed-off shotgun first. It was a Remington, the barrel hacked off with a saw, the grooves of the teeth still visible against the metal. It was a useful find, devastating at close range. The buckshot could rip a man like canvas and blow hinges off doors.

A very useful find.

She took out the Beretta next. It was small and sleek, polymer and steel, with no protrusions to snag against clothes if it was carried in a pocket. It had low-profile sights and bevelled edges. There was no slide to be seen, and the reversible mag release was the pistol's only raised feature.

She checked to make sure it was unloaded and handed it to Isabella.

"This is yours," she said. "It's smaller than the ones you've been practicing with, but it's compact and easy to carry. Easy to hide, too. Six rounds in the magazine and one in the chamber, so you can't fire without thinking. You've got to be accurate."

She took out the box of ammunition, Federal Champion 115gr FMJ, and gave it to Isabella to load the magazine.

Her daughter held it in her hand and assessed it.

"What do you think?"

"It's small."

"Still packs a punch. Treat it with respect."

She watched as Isabella field-stripped the pistol, checking the workings and then assembling it again.

"It's new," she said.

"As good as."

Jimmy Kimmel was on the TV. Beatrix found the remote and switched off the set.

"It's late," she said.

"When do we get started?"

"Tomorrow," Beatrix replied. "It's a big day. We need to sleep."

Chapter Nine

S he had wanted to start first thing in the morning, but the day dawned bright and clear, and to her surprise, she felt better than she had for days. It could only be a temporary thing, but it gave her a jolt of optimism, and she decided that she should take advantage of it.

She didn't have many days left to her, and the days that she would actually be able to enjoy numbered even less.

Isabella was just starting to rouse in the bed next to her, and so she quickly used the bathroom and then dressed for the day.

"Hello, sweetheart," she said as the girl blinked away the grogginess of waking.

"Hello, Mummy."

"Sleep well?"

"Yes. What are we doing?"

"Up you get."

"Are we going out?"

"You want to look around New York, don't you?"

She had left the Impala in the hotel garage. It would be safe there. She was confident that it was stolen, and anyway, how likely was it that someone involved in the drug trade would report the theft of a car that they themselves had likely stolen? And even if it wasn't stolen and they did report it, the garage of one of the most expensive hotels in Manhattan would have been at the bottom of the list of places that the police would think to look.

Yes, she thought. It was safe.

They filled their day to the brim, as much as Beatrix's health allowed. They started in Central Park, visiting the Belvedere Castle, the Friedsam Memorial and the Sheep Meadow. They took taxis south, stopping at Carnegie Hall, the Rockefeller Center and the Chrysler Building, and then followed FDR Drive all the way down to the Brooklyn Bridge. They rode along Wall Street, then into Battery Park, then stopped at the 9/11 Memorial. They ate hot dogs from a street vendor and then took the ferry to Ellis Island and gazed up at Lady Liberty. They returned to Manhattan and spent a lost hour in the vastness of Macy's, with Beatrix buying her daughter a three-hundred-dollar jacket that she obviously liked, but was too polite to ask for. They drank coffee and ate pastries and then, as dusk approached, cut northeast until they were in Times Square. Beatrix was dog tired, but there was one more thing that she wanted to do. They followed the crowds, the massive digital billboards throwing a changing wash of neon across the gridlocked cars and taxis that jostled for position, and stopped to laugh at the hawkers and hucksters, pushing their tawdry art on credulous tourists. Isabella tugged Beatrix across the road to the huge McDonald's. They passed beneath the enormous red and yellow arches and went inside. They ate cheeseburgers and fries, drank Cokes and then ventured out into the clamour and bustle again.

"Where now?" Isabella asked.

Beatrix looked up at the sky; it was dark enough now.

"Come on," she said. "There's somewhere I've always wanted to go."

They took a taxi a half mile along Seventh Avenue, then along West 34th Street, turning onto Fifth Avenue and then, finally, West 33rd Street.

Isabella looked up.

"That's the Empire State Building, isn't it?"

Beatrix smiled.

They looked up at the building as it stretched overhead.

"It's beautiful," the girl said.

"You want to go up?"

She beamed. "Can we?"

"Of course. Come on."

They went inside the art deco lobby with the two Stars and Stripes that hung from poles attached to brackets in the wall. Beatrix paid their entrance fees, and they waited for the elevator. A sign on the wall said that visibility was good for twenty-five miles in daylight and that there was a light breeze. They rode up the first lift, changed at the mid-point, boarded another and climbed all the way to the eighty-sixth floor.

"My ears are popping," Isabella said with a wide smile.

"Mine too."

"Have you done this before?"

"No," she said. "I never have."

Isabella held onto Beatrix's hand the whole way and squeezed tighter as they waited to shuffle out onto the observation deck. They moved to the edge, gripping onto the guard rails that stretched up and then curved back over them.

The view was astonishing from a quarter mile up. The island of Manhattan, set like a jewel amid its nest of blackly glittering waters, stared up at them: the needling skyscrapers, all lit up, the roads that looked like ravines, the traffic so small and pointless, the wide green swatch of Central Park. Over there was the Hudson, more like the flash of a sword blade than a noble river. From here, they could see that the city was not the infinite succession of canyons that they might have supposed, and to which their feet and legs bore witness, but that it had limits, fading away into the curtains of darkness that were the waters that bordered it on all sides before the renewed glitter of Union City, Newark and Queens.

It seemed right, somehow, that the first time she saw this view was with Isabella.

She felt her daughter's hand as it slipped into her palm again. She was dizzy with pain and fatigue, and closed her fingers around it, squeezing tight.

She looked across at her.

"Are you alright?" she asked her daughter.

Isabella squeezed her hand in response. "You know I love you, Mummy?"

Beatrix's heart felt thick and heavy, and she felt an ache in the pit of her stomach.

She remembered feeling like that, before, years ago.

A lifetime ago.

She had discounted the possibility that she would ever feel that way again.

"I love you too, Bella."

Low clouds darted and scudded across the sky, seemingly close enough to touch.

"Have you had a good day?"

"Yes," she said. "I . . . I . . ."

"What is it?"

"Mummy," she began again, hesitantly.

"Yes?"

"I know you're ill."

Beatrix stopped, unsure of how she should answer. She had never mentioned her sickness to Isabella. That didn't mean that it was something that she could easily hide. She supposed that the girl would have had to have her eyes closed not to notice that something was wrong with her mother. She had been exhausted this afternoon and unable to keep the flickers of pain from her face. Isabella's life had been awful, and Beatrix hadn't wanted to burden her with the grim certainty that it hadn't yet plumbed its full depths. She could see now that she needn't have worried. She had known, anyway.

"I have cancer," she said. "Do you know what that means?"

"Is it very bad?"

"Yes," she said. "Very bad."

"Will you . . . ?"

"Yes," she said with a catch in her voice. "I don't have very much time left."

The girl looked out over the marvellous tapestry laid out before them. Her eyes started to fill and she blinked furiously, trying to stop the tears, but they came anyway.

Beatrix felt her own eyes filling. "I'm sorry, sweetheart."

She gulped for air. "But we only . . . it was only last year."

"I know."

"It's not fair."

"No."

Isabella breathed quickly, mastering the emotion, her lip still quivering.

It *wasn't* fair. When she had been diagnosed in Hong Kong, she hadn't cared. In a perverse way, she had welcomed it. She thought that she had nothing to live for, and it was an exit for her, a way out. That was the reason that she had done almost nothing at all to fight it. She had been chasing oblivion, and this was just another, albeit more permanent, kind. It just seemed easier to close her eyes, spread her arms wide and embrace it.

But things were different now.

"I'm sorry," Beatrix said again.

Isabella raised her chin, her wet eyes shining in the lights from the streets below. "The ones who did what they did. To Daddy. And to you."

"There's only one of them left, Bella."

"And you'll get him?"

"Yes," she said. "I will."

Chapter Ten

The New York Ballet Company had its headquarters in the Lincoln Center on the Upper West Side. It was a sleek and smart area of town, with a host of high-end eateries and bars serving the patrons who flocked to enjoy the arts each evening. Beatrix slid out of the traffic and parked the Impala at the side of the road, next to the long flight of steps that led up to the wide square, the illuminated fountain and the main buildings that were set around it.

She turned off the engine and turned to Isabella.

"Are you alright?" she asked.

"Yes," her daughter replied. She was trying to hide her nerves.

"You're going to be fine," Beatrix said, her hand on the girl's shoulder.

"I can do it."

"I know you can, Bella. Are you ready?"

"Yes."

"You've got the picture?"

She held up one of the two smartphones they had just bought. She scrubbed a finger against the screen and brought up the picture of the pretty young girl, eighteen or nineteen years old, that they had downloaded from the ballet company's website. "There."

"That's good."

"And you know where to wait?"

"The stage door. I know."

"Call me when you know where she's going. Alright?"

Beatrix would have preferred to do it herself, of course, but she was in so much pain now that she wasn't sure that she would be able to walk at a normal pace for long. And there was the possibility that Control had warned his children what she looked like. This was important and if their presence was revealed, the game would be up.

Isabella had to do it. It was her, or not at all.

"Okay," the girl said. She opened the door and the cold air washed inside.

"You'll do great," Beatrix said.

Isabella closed the door. Beatrix watched as she looked left and right, crossed the sidewalk and then climbed the steps. She was absorbed into the crowd before she had gained the second flight.

Beatrix started the car and pulled back out into the flow of traffic again.

Isabella walked into the wide square that lay between the buildings that made up this cultural quarter of New York. It was scrupulously clean and tidy, and she couldn't help but make the comparison with the main square in Marrakech, that seething, confused and throbbing mass of humanity that cooked under the burning desert sun. This space, with its scrubbed-clean flagstones, its pristine signage and its raised beds with ordered planting, was sterile and antiseptic. Isabella knew which she preferred.

She hurried across the square to the entrance of the building that she wanted. There was an alleyway that led around to the rear, and she made her way quickly down it. The stage door was at the end of the corridor. It had been left open, but a sign tacked to it advised that access was for company members only. A bored member of the staff sat in a booth, checking credentials against a list on a computer screen.

Isabella walked by the door. The alleyway opened out onto a road, and there was a bench on the broad sidewalk next to a bus stop. She turned and leaned against it. It offered a clear view into the alleyway all the way to the stage door. She closed her coat around her and settled there to wait.

The company's rehearsals finished thirty minutes later, and the men and women started to filter out of the stage door. The dancers were the easiest to distinguish: the men were tall and lithe, the women slender and delicate. Isabella waited and watched. Some of the dancers came and waited by her bus stop, climbed aboard the waiting buses and disappeared away to do whatever it was they had planned for the rest of the afternoon.

Cassidy Fields, Control's daughter, was one of the last to emerge. Isabella recognised her at once. She was tall and thin, with glossy hair that reached down to her shoulder blades and skin that was so clear and fresh that it almost shimmered with health. She was wearing a leather jacket and a beanie on her head. Isabella was certain that it was her, but she still took the iPhone from her pocket and scrolled through the pictures to be sure.

Yes, it was her. There was no question about it.

The girl was with two others, both of the same build and both likewise shining with health and happiness. They came over to the bus stop and waited. Isabella shuffled across the seat so that she was a little closer to them. They were talking about one of the choreographers, a man who, so they said, had a reputation for lechery.

A bus drew up, its hydraulic brakes sighing as it slowed and stopped.

The door rattled as it slid open.

Cassidy said goodbye to the other girls. The pair climbed aboard, paid their fare and moved down into the bus. She waved as the bus drew away, her friends returning the farewell.

Cassidy set off to the north.

Isabella followed. She stayed twenty feet back, just like her mother had taught her. Close enough that it would be difficult to lose the target, but not so close that she would give herself away.

They walked for ten minutes until Cassidy reached the entrance to the subway station at 66th St/Lincoln Center Station. She turned off the sidewalk and went into the subway.

Isabella followed.

Cassidy ambled down to the platform, and as a train drew alongside, stepped into the empty carriage. She sat and Isabella did the same at the opposite end of the carriage. A newspaper had been discarded on the seat next to her, and she picked it up and pretended to read, watching Cassidy over the top of the paper.

72nd Street.

79th Street.

86th Street.

91st Street.

She showed no sign of getting off.

181st Street.

191st Street.

Dyckman Street.

The further to the north they travelled, the more alone and vulnerable Isabella felt.

207th Street.

215th Street.

She took out the cellphone and rubbed her finger along its metallic edge. She had to fight the urge to get off the train, give up, call her mother to come and pick her up.

Marble Hill.

231st Street.

238th Street.

The train drew to a stop at Van Cortlandt Park. Cassidy, who had been distracted by her book, looked up and, with alarm that switched into self-conscious amusement, got to her feet and hurried out of the carriage. Isabella did the same, exiting onto the platform just as the doors had started to close. The train exhaled and then rattled away into the dark maw of the tunnel.

Isabella had no idea where she was. The station was suburban, a terminus on the line and an entrance to the commuter belt that encircled the outskirts of the city. It was quieter than the others that they had passed through on their journey north. She looked around: there were advertising hoardings on the pillars that supported the roof; a busker playing a penny whistle, with a cap laid out before his crossed legs; a blind man with a cane, tapping out an uncertain route to the stairs.

Cassidy pressed her earbuds into her ears and dipped her head to the rhythm of whatever it was she was listening to as she climbed the stairs to street level. She pressed her electronic ticket to the sensor, stepped through the gates and exited onto the dark street outside.

Isabella did the same.

Chapter Eleven

Beatrix followed Isabella's directions, heading north, driving quickly, but carefully. She pulled up to the kerb, parked and killed the lights. She had never been to the Van Cortlandt Park area before, and she felt uncomfortable. The area was etched into the hill that descended from the Jerome Park Reservoir and offered a terraced niche of narrow, winding streets. It was tranquil, with plenty of trees and tended gardens, and neo-Tudor and neo-Georgian houses cheek by jowl with large brick apartment buildings.

She looked anxiously up and down the street. She couldn't see Isabella for a moment, but then suddenly she saw a flash of motion in the wing mirror as her daughter jogged across the sidewalk, opened the door and slid inside.

"Are you alright?"

"Yes," she said. "I'm fine."

"How was it?"

"It was alright."

"Where did she go?"

"She went into that building," she said, pointing across the street to a three-storey brownstone that had been turned into apartments.

"Do you know which one?"

"I watched. The light in the second one came on after she went inside. It was off before."

"Good girl," Beatrix said.

"Did I do okay?"

"You did better than okay."

"What now?"

Beatrix reached over, opened the glove box and took out the Beretta. She shoved it into the pocket of her leather jacket.

"Mummy?"

"We need her for what we need to do," she said. "Will you wait here for me?"

"Yes."

"If you see anyone going into the building, call me."

"I will."

She crossed the sidewalk and walked the thirty yards to the brownstone. She felt as if she had been hollowed out, all her strength sucked away, and she took two morphine tablets from her pocket and swallowed them dry. She didn't think they would serve much use when her body was screaming at her to rest, but maybe it would be better than nothing.

She waited at the foot of the steps into the building, out of sight, until she was as confident as she could be that she was not being watched, and then struggled up the steps to the door. She took the small flathead screwdriver that she had purchased while Isabella was tracking the girl and slid the point into the door jamb just below the handle. She gave it a quick, firm yank towards her, and the bolt splintered through the wooden box and the door swung open.

She entered a lobby. There was a door to the apartment on the ground floor and a wide staircase that climbed to the first and second floors. She started up the stairs, her hand in her pocket resting loosely around the handle of the handgun.

She reached the first floor. There was a door with the number 2 on it. The landing was dark, and a strip of golden light shone out of the narrow gap between the bottom of the door and the floor.

Her telephone vibrated. She put it to her ear.

"Bella?" she whispered.

"Someone's coming in."

Beatrix looked quickly to the left and right. There were no other doors on the landing and nowhere to hide.

She heard a muffled exclamation of surprise from below as whoever was entering noticed that the lock had been broken.

Beatrix followed the landing around and climbed halfway up the next flight of stairs. She would be invisible to anyone coming up as long as they went no farther than the door to flat two. If they were headed for the second upper floor, there would be nowhere for her to hide.

She heard the footsteps as someone climbed up to the first floor.

She took out the handgun.

The footsteps reached the half landing and kept coming.

She held the gun straight, aiming down to the half landing.

She heard a knock on the door.

She breathed out.

The door opened.

"Hey, Joel," came a woman's voice.

"You've got a problem, Cassy," Joel answered. "Front door's been forced."

"It was alright when I came in."

"When was that?"

"Fifteen minutes ago."

"You think someone was locked out?"

"I didn't see anyone."

"Then someone's broken in."

There was a pause. "You think I should call the cops? What should I do?"

Beatrix stood, a little too quickly, and put out an arm against the banister to ward off the dizziness.

Not now.

———⌣———

She breathed in and out, gathering her strength, and then descended. She turned on the half landing and kept going down. Cassidy Fields was in the doorway of her apartment. A tall bearded man, handsome and muscular, was facing Cassidy. That was Joel.

"Inside," Beatrix said in a flat and emotionless voice.

"Who . . ." Cassidy began. She lost her words as Beatrix waved the gun at her.

Panic filled her face.

Joel turned.

"Inside."

"She's got a gun," Cassidy said.

Beatrix reached the landing and flicked the gun towards the door. Cassidy backed up. Beatrix extended her arm, jabbing the gun at Joel's face, and he side-stepped inside, too. Beatrix followed, shutting the door behind her.

She looked around quickly. She was in a small hallway. Doors led off it. One of them was open, and she saw the end of a bed.

"In there," she said, pointing to the bedroom.

"What is this?"

"Into the bedroom. Now."

They both did as they were told, backing inside, their hands held up before them. Beatrix followed.

"Take off your belt," she said to Joel.

"Take off my . . . ?"

"Take off your belt," she said, her voice still calm, yet laced with threat. She turned to Cassidy and pointed to a canvas sack with a long strap that had been dumped on the bed. "Give me the strap from that bag."

She collected the belt and the strap.

"Lie down," she ordered.

Cassidy started down to her knees.

"Not you," she said. "Just him. You sit down on the bed and don't move."

Joel did as she said. She told him to turn around, and he did. She told him to put his hands behind his back, and he did. She quickly looped the belt around his ankles, knotted it and yanked it tight. She took the strap and knotted it around his wrists, taking the long end and knotting it into the belt until he was hog-tied.

"What are you doing?" Cassidy said.

"Be quiet."

"I haven't got any money."

"I don't want money."

"Then what . . . ?"

"Listen very carefully," she cut across her. "I don't want to hurt you, either of you, and I won't if you do exactly what I tell you to do. But if you do anything stupid, you'll be shot, and that's a promise. Do you understand me?"

"Yes," she said.

"Good. I need you to come with me. I have a car outside. You're going to go downstairs first, and I'm going to be right behind you. Close behind you, too close to miss if you do anything other than exactly what I say. You're going to open the door, go down the steps, go onto the street and get into the back of the car."

"What for? I don't . . ."

"We're just going to go for a drive. And I promise you won't be harmed if you do what I tell you. Understand?"

"Yes."

"And you," she said, looking down at Joel, "I want you to stay here, nice and quiet. Remember, I've got Cassidy with me, and I don't want any distractions from the police. When we're outside the city, I'll call them and let them know what's happened. They'll come and untie you. Do you understand?"

"Why are you doing this? We're just normal people."

She stared at him, hard. "I need you to tell me that you understand."

"Yes, of course I fucking understand."

"Okay. That's good."

She took out her phone and sent the text that she had already prepared.

Start the car.

She pointed to the hook by the door. "Get your hat and coat."

Cassidy took a knitted beanie and a leather jacket and put them on.

"Let's go."

She took the girl by the arm and propelled her gently to the door.

"What he said was right," Cassidy said, turning her head to look back at her. "We're just normal people. I'm just a dancer. I don't have any money. I don't know . . ."

"Concentrate on getting down to the car in one piece, please, Cassidy."

"How do you know my name?"

"Down the stairs."

They descended to the half landing and then kept going down. The door had swung open, and, outside, Beatrix heard the buzz and electricity of the city. She heard a siren wailing in the distance. Nothing to do with them, she knew, although that would change soon enough.

They descended the steps to the sidewalk, Beatrix walking alongside Cassidy like they were best friends. Her left hand touched the girl's arm. Her right held the gun, hidden in her sleeve.

"It's the Impala," she said, indicating the car. The lights were burning, and the engine was running. "Inside."

Cassidy opened the rear door and slid inside. Beatrix shut the door after her. She got into the front. Isabella was in the passenger seat. Beatrix handed the gun to her.

"Cover her until we're out of the city," she said.

Her daughter turned in the passenger seat and held the Beretta in steady hands.

Beatrix released the handbrake, put the car into drive, and pulled into traffic.

Chapter Twelve

Beatrix drove for two hours straight. It was a struggle, and by the time they were out past Philadelphia, she knew that she needed to stop. She found a drive-thru McDonald's and pulled into the parking lot. She slid into an empty space at the back of the lot, away from the other cars, and switched off the engine. She squeezed her hands into fists as the pain washed over her.

"Mummy?" Isabella asked.

She closed her eyes until the pain relented. "I'm fine, Bella," she said. "Are you hungry?"

"I guess."

She turned and looked back at Cassidy. "You hungry?"

"Yes."

"What do you want?"

"I don't know. Burger and fries. Diet Coke."

She took a twenty from her pocket and gave it to Isabella. "Go and get a burger and fries and whatever you want."

"What about you?"

"I'll just have a coffee."

"You don't want to eat?"

Her stomach felt like liquid, and the prospect revolted her. "I'm fine. Just a cup of coffee for me. Make it strong."

Isabella gave her a look of concern but left the car and headed for the bright lights of the restaurant. Beatrix watched her in the rearview until she had disappeared inside.

She refocused and looked at Cassidy. She was extraordinarily pretty, with a delicate and slender face that looked like it belonged in a Renaissance painting. She was slender, like Isabella, and Beatrix doubted if there was even an ounce of fat on her. Everything was graceful and precise: her movements, the line of her eyebrows, the shine of her fingernails. Beatrix found it difficult to credit that her father was the man that she knew him to be. It seemed inconceivable that such a man, both morally and physically repellent, could have produced such a jewel.

"Are you alright?" Beatrix asked her.

"What do you think?"

"I'm sorry."

"Sorry?"

"I'm sorry that this is necessary."

"That *what* is necessary? You haven't said a thing. I don't understand what's happening."

"You're not going to be harmed."

"Says the woman with the fucking gun."

"This doesn't have anything to do with you."

"Then what *does* it have to do with?"

"Have you spoken to your father recently?"

"No. Not for a month. Maybe more. Is this about him?"

"Yes."

"You know him?"

"I do."

"So . . . ?"

"We have some things we need to talk about."

"You didn't think about just giving him a call?"

"He doesn't want to speak to me."

"How can I help with that?"

"You'll get his attention. Once that's done, you can go. You have my word."

There was a moment of silence as Cassidy brooded in the back. Beatrix watched the streaming traffic on the freeway and, overhead, the blinking lights of a passenger jet.

"Where are you taking me?" Cassidy asked.

"We're going to see him."

"He's in the country?"

"You don't know?"

"He moves around a lot."

"Since when?"

"Recently. I never know where he is from day to day."

"He tell you why that was?"

"Business. We don't talk about it."

"He's here on the East Coast. North Carolina. We're going there."

———

The pain, in some ways, was helpful. It made it less likely that she would drift off to sleep at the wheel, but there were still moments when she found it almost impossible to resist the downward tug of her eyelids, as if they had been hung with weights. They were just outside Pocomoke, Maryland, when she was jarred awake by an angry blast from the horn of an eighteen-wheeler. She opened her eyes to find her chin on her chest. They had been drifting across to the middle of the road, and she had swung the wheel hard to put them right, the lights of the big truck flashing by them. Isabella and Cassidy were asleep and did not awaken. Beatrix focussed on the ache in her bones once again.

They were close now, just two hours away.

Nearly there.

She followed US Route 13 down towards Chesapeake Bay, crossed the bridge and arrived at her destination a little after three in the morning.

It was good timing: Beatrix could barely hold her eyes open, and if there had been just another half an hour to travel, she had decided that they would have had to sleep in the car. She had researched the place she wanted to stay while they were at the St Regis, before they had collected Cassidy. There was a holiday village eighteen miles to the northwest of Chesapeake. It was a series of cabins set in the woods, nice and remote, none of them too close to another. She had booked them in for a week, although they wouldn't need that long. It would be perfect.

She turned off the interstate, followed Portsmouth Boulevard west and drove until she reached the turnoff. She parked in the lot next to the reception. She had called ahead for the keys to be left for them, and she sent Isabella inside to get them while she stayed with Cassidy in the car.

"Everything alright?" she asked as her daughter got back into the Impala.

"No problem."

They followed a long, winding, single-lane track that was asphalted only for the first quarter mile. She drove carefully, the Impala bumping up and down, the headlights swooping between the trunks of the trees.

Their cabin was at the end of the lane on the banks of a large lake. The owner had left the lights on, and puddles of golden warmth spilled out across a wooden veranda.

She parked outside the door.

"No scenes," she warned Cassidy as she switched off the engine. "You saw how isolated this is. We're in the middle of nowhere. No one would hear a thing, and you'd just put me in a bad mood. We go in, nice and quiet, and then we can get some sleep. This will all be over tomorrow. Do you understand?"

The young woman nodded resentfully.

Beatrix stepped out of the car. The night air was crisp and refreshing, and her tiredness was temporarily beaten back. Isabella got out, unlocked the cabin door, opened the trunk and ferried their bags inside. Beatrix opened the rear door and took Cassidy's elbow as she slid out. She walked her quickly inside and then returned to the car. She took the length of rope that she had purchased at the same time as the screwdriver, went back to the veranda, turned to blip the Impala's locks and then went inside and closed and locked the door.

The cabin was reasonably large. There was a sitting room with a log burner, and a kitchenette and a single bedroom. The embers of a fire were glowing in the grate, and Isabella went over and dropped two logs onto it. They caught quickly, orange flames hungrily spreading across the dry wood.

Beatrix uncurled the rope.

"What?" Cassidy exclaimed, pointing. "What the fuck?"

"We all need to rest," Beatrix explained. "If I were you, I'd wait until everyone else was asleep, and then I'd make a run for it. I can't have you doing that. This is to make sure you don't. It's just for tonight."

"This is ridiculous," the girl said, but she didn't resist and allowed Beatrix to shepherd her into the bedroom. She looped the rope around the girl's wrists, fastening it with a constrictor knot, and then knotted the other end to the wooden headboard. There was enough play on the rope for her to be comfortable, but not enough for her to get out of the room.

"Lie down," Beatrix said. She pointed to the bed. "The side away from the door."

She did.

Beatrix turned to Isabella. "Lie down next to her."

"No," she said. "I can sleep on the floor. You sleep on the bed."

"I'm alright, Bella. I'll sleep in the chair outside."

Isabella looked reluctant, but she relented.

She smiled at her daughter. "Get some sleep. Tomorrow is going to be a big day."

Chapter Thirteen

Beatrix woke at five as the dawn light played in through the window. She had forgotten to close the drapes. The fire had died overnight, and the room was a little cold. Her muscles and bones screamed in protest as she levered herself upright. She paused, assessing herself. The usual wave of nausea passed through her, radiating out from the pit of her stomach, but it dissipated without gathering strength. After a minute, she felt confident enough to arise. She negotiated the room carefully, one hand pressed up against the log wall, and quietly closed the drapes.

Isabella and Cassidy were asleep. She took a homespun blanket from a wooden chest and arranged it carefully over them both. Isabella moaned and twitched, but she did not awaken.

Beatrix went into the bathroom and ran a bath. She stripped off her clothes and stared at her reflection in the mirror. The cancer was eating her from the inside. She had always been slender, but now she looked emaciated. Her ribcage was visible, and the points of her elbows and shoulders were obscenely sharp. She turned to look at the four roses that she had had tattooed on her arm. There was space for another two and, if she had had time, she would have returned to Johnny Ink and had the fifth, for Connor English, etched into her skin. But there had been no time, and his passing had not been recorded. There would be no sixth for Control, either, whatever happened tomorrow.

She leaned in closer. The work had been pristine when she'd had it done, but there had been more flesh on her bones then. She had lost muscle even in the short interval after her return from Iraq. Duffy's rose, which had been full and ripe, now looked shrivelled and wrinkled. The others were the same. The scarlet petals were shrinking and dying, just as she was.

———

Beatrix felt a little better when she got out of the bath half an hour later. She heard the sound of movement outside, and as she dressed in a pair of jeans and a black T-shirt, there came a gentle knocking at the door.

"It's open."

Isabella pushed it open.

"Did I wake you?" she asked the girl.

"No."

"Did you sleep well?"

"It was alright."

Beatrix towelled her hair dry and combed out the tangles.

"What are we doing today?" Isabella asked her.

"I have to go and buy some things."

"Do you want me to come, too?"

"No, I need you to stay here, Bella." She nodded in the direction of the bedroom, where she could hear Cassidy stirring. "We can't let her outside. Not even for a minute. If anyone sees her, this all comes to an end. I need you to stay here with her and make sure she doesn't leave."

"How?"

"We'll let her use the bathroom, and then I'll tie her to the bed again. If she makes any noise, there's no one outside to hear her. And I'll leave the pistol with you, too. Just in case."

"I'd have to shoot her?"

Beatrix's conscience flared at the thought of it. "You won't have to."

"But if she got away from me?"

"She won't, Bella."

Isabella glanced over at the pistol on the table and frowned.

"How long will you be?"

"Just the morning. I know what I need, and I know exactly where to get it."

"Hey," came a call from the bedroom. *"Hey."*

Beatrix went over to the doorway, fetching the Beretta as she passed the table. Cassidy was sitting on the edge of the bed, the tether stretched taut.

"I need to . . . you know . . . I need to pee."

Beatrix made sure the girl could see the pistol and then unfastened the knot, leaving it tied to the bedstead.

"Come on, then," she said, taking her by the arm and leading her to the bathroom.

Cassidy stepped inside. Beatrix followed close enough behind to block the door with her foot when she tried to close it.

"A little privacy?"

"No. Door stays open. Do what you have to do."

"Jesus," the girl said, exasperated. She lowered her trousers and sat down.

Beatrix backed away so that she could maintain her modesty. "You're going to stay in the bedroom this morning," Beatrix said to her in a tone that brooked no contradiction. "I'm not going to be far away. If you do anything stupid, and I mean *anything*, I'll be back here before you know it. If you do as I say, we'll be out of your way by this time tomorrow. Understand?" The girl grunted. "That going to be a problem, Cassidy?"

"Do I have any choice?"

"Not really."

"Then why did you bother to ask me?" She stood, washed and dried her hands and then presented them to her again. "Go on, then. You better tie me up."

Beatrix did, and then she took Isabella out into the main room again.

"Are you going to be alright?" she asked her.

"Yes," the girl said, firmly.

"Here." She handed her the Beretta. "Just knowing that you have it should keep her quiet. You won't need to use it."

"Just the morning?"

"Just the morning. As quick as I can."

***

She drove into town. Her first stop was at the Chesapeake Square Mall in Virginia. She parked the Impala and went inside. It was early; the shops were only just opening, and there were just a few people there. She asked for directions and followed them to Radio Shack. She knew it would be stocked with everything that she would need. She nodded to the greeter and, collecting a wire mesh basket, worked her way around the aisles in search of the items on her list: a toggle switch, a push switch, a 5mm LED, mono audio jacks, phone plugs, soldering iron and solder, intercom wire, snap connectors, eight AA batteries and a battery holder, alligator clips and a roll of nichrome wire. She added a screwdriver set, wire cutters and a drill with various bits. Finally, she added a Samsung prepaid phone and a windscreen mount.

She paid, bagged the items, thanked the girl on the till and took them outside to the Impala. She got inside and fired up the phone, bringing up the internet and searching for locations where she could get the other items on her list.

There were several places that looked promising.

She copied the address of the first stop and pasted it into the mapping app. She slotted the phone into the mount, stuck it to the window and waited as it generated directions.

She fired up the engine and drew away, turning to the west and driving back out of town.

———

The things Beatrix needed to buy were not the kinds of things that someone like her would be expected to need and certainly not in the quantities that she had in mind.

She had to be careful.

The most important thing was fertiliser. There was a Southern States farm co-op on the outskirts of Chesapeake. She knew that she wouldn't be able to buy more than a couple of bags without encouraging questions that she wouldn't be able to answer, and so she heaved two twenty-five pound sacks into her cart and wheeled them to the checkout. The clerk asked for her identification, and Beatrix pulled out the fake driving license that she had brought with her from Morocco.

The woman lowered her glasses and squinted at the picture, then back up at Beatrix.

She smiled sweetly at her.

"What are you going to be using this for, ma'am?"

"Horses," she explained. "The waste from the stables. You stir this in with the wood shavings and the manure, and it composts twice as fast."

"It surely will," the woman said. "Sorry for asking."

"It's alright."

"We have to be so careful these days." She cocked an eyebrow at her and said, in a tone of great opprobrium, "Terrorists. You can make a mighty big bang with a few bags of this."

"So I hear."

A staff member helped her to load the fertiliser into the trunk of the Impala. She thanked him and set off again.

She scrolled through her notes and selected the second waypoint, continuing west until she reached the hardware store near Lake Cavalier. It was a friendly mom-and-pop kind of place, and she walked the aisles and selected two twenty-five-litre polyethylene tubs and four large bottles of commercial cleansing solution with liquid nitromethane. The owner talked to her about the weather as she settled up her bill.

The next place was another farm store in Portsmouth. She bought two more big bags of fertiliser, stowing those on the back seats.

She drove to the fourth destination, following the back roads for another hour until she had found a suitably quiet gas station. She parked next to the pump, took the nozzle and filled the Impala's tank to the brim. Then she went around to the trunk and, ensuring that she wasn't observed, pumped another five gallons of fuel into each of the tubs, sealing them with the airtight lids.

The pain and fatigue started to mount, but she was done. She paid the attendant, bought a bottle of water and a packet of gum, and set off again, heading back to the camp. She had been out for just over three hours, but she had everything she needed.

She rolled the car to a stop, crunching the tires in the gravel that covered the road. She was apprehensive as she opened the door and stepped outside. Isabella was a capable girl, but she knew that she was asking a lot of her. The year that she had spent training her had several aims. She wanted her to be able to fire a range of weapons, defend herself, be fit and strong. One of its main goals, the least tangible one, had been to impart a streetwise edge to her that was beyond her years. She had been only partially successful in that. It was a testament to her daughter's character that she retained her innocence, just below the surface, despite it all. In some ways, she had been pleased that she had failed in that regard, but now, as she stepped up onto the porch, she hoped that had not been a liability that would put her in harm's way.

The door was closed. She turned the handle and pushed it open. "Isabella?"

"In here," she said.

Beatrix went inside. The girl had turned one of the chairs around so that she could sit and face the door to the bedroom. She went closer and looked down to see the Beretta resting in her lap.

"Is everything alright?"

"I'm fine," she said.

"She give you any trouble?"

"Tried to get me to untie her, but I said I wouldn't."

"Good girl," Beatrix said, relieved. She leaned down and kissed her on the top of the head. The movement elicited a jolt of pain, and she winced, glad that her daughter was facing away and couldn't see it.

She took the pistol and went into the bedroom. Cassidy was sitting on the bed, her back resting against the headboard and her knees clutched up tight against her chest.

"You're back," the girl said sourly.

"I am."

"Are you going to untie me?"

"Yes," she said, reaching down and releasing the rope. "This is nearly over for you."

"Really? Any reason I should believe that?"

"No. But it is. There's just one thing I want you to do."

"What?"

"I want you to call your father."

"And say what?"

"The truth. Tell him what's happened to you. Tell him you're with me."

"What do I call you? I don't know your name."

"I'm Beatrix. He'll know who I am. But don't try and tell him where we are. I don't want you to try and give him even the slightest clue. That will just make me angry, and it's not in your interest to do that. You'll be on with him for fifteen seconds maximum, and then you'll give the phone to me." She looked at her hard, staring right into her eyes. "Can you do that for me, Cassidy?"

"Sure. Fine. Give me a phone."

Beatrix took out the burner phone she had purchased in Radio Shack, powered it up and gave it to her. She took the pistol and rested it in her lap. "Remember. Don't try anything stupid."

Cassidy blanched, looked down at the phone and started to tap out numbers.

Chapter Fourteen

Control sat at the glass conference table, only half focussed on the presentation that was being delivered. The meeting was not a happy occasion. Beatrix Rose had caused Manage Risk almost incalculable damage in Iraq, and the discussion had been scheduled so that they could try and take stock and consider their next move.

The senior management of the company were all present. One of the intelligence officers had been given the onerous task of recapping the situation, and he did so carefully and precisely, warily sending glances to the head of the table where Jamie King brooded quietly.

Control was wearily familiar with it. There had been a problem with one of the operatives, Mackenzie West, who they had employed down there. They got it wrong now and again, and this was one of those occasions. The man, an ex-soldier who now professed something so foolish as a conscience, had threatened to go public after witnessing a riot that had left protesters dead after Manage Risk attempted to disperse it. They had become aware that he was unstable and had detained him for "medical evaluation," although that was a bland euphemism for dropping him in a dark box until they worked out the best way to neutralise him.

He had been broken out of custody and spirited away into Kuwait.

Control could detect the hand of British intelligence from a mile away.

It was the kind of operation he himself would have attempted when he was in command of Group Fifteen. His successor, Michael Pope, had enjoyed an auspicious coup.

"And if he gives evidence against us?" King asked.

"The case would have to go against us first."

"And if it did?"

"The Iraqis will cancel the contract and put it back out to tender."

"Can we persuade them that they have overreacted?"

The man shook his head.

"How much will that cost us?" King demanded.

"The contract is for twenty-five million," the chief financial officer reported.

"Twenty-five!"

"It's not just *our* contract, Jamie," the woman responsible for government affairs said. "It's everything. The oilfield will be back in play again, and that's worth *billions* in taxes. I've had heat from the White House and the Treasury, and that's without even mentioning the shit I'm getting practically every hour from the oil companies."

"What kind of shit?"

"The shit where they say Hell will freeze over before they ever think about working with us again."

"Legal exposure?" King asked, looking to the lawyer.

The man tapped his pencil against the table. "The State Department have said they'll revoke our licence to operate over there. That's not a bluff. Justice is talking about opening a prosecution against us. My source says the FBI have already spoken to West. Two agents flew out to Kuwait. We managed to fight it off last time, but that was without this new evidence. It'll be more difficult now. And those are corporate charges. They could affect all of us."

"What do you mean?"

"Personal liability, Jamie. Fines. Custodial sentences, even."

King swivelled to Control. "That fucking woman," he said. "That's one expensive grudge." His tone was jovial, but there was an edge behind it that Control did not misunderstand.

The discussion moved on to the financial implications of the incident. The stock market had yet to hear of the scale of the problem, but the consensus was that investors would be spooked, and unless they moved decisively, it could spark a run on their shares. If that happened, there was a chance that the banks would take fright and start to call in their loans. That, in turn, could give their customers a reason to kill their deals. All of their key contracts had termination provisions that could be triggered in the event of doubts over the company's solvency. It wasn't difficult to see what might very easily happen if they did not force the situation back under control: one consequence would trigger another and another, like falling dominos, and there was no way of telling how much damage might eventually be caused. The whole company could be at stake.

Control was staring disconsolately at the doodles he had made in the margins of his notepad, when his phone started to vibrate on the table.

Only a tiny handful of people knew the number.

He took it quickly and checked the display.

Unknown caller.

"I'm sorry," he said. "I have to take this."

King glared at him.

He put the phone to his ear.

"Hello?"

"Daddy?"

He frowned. "Cassy?"

"Daddy!"

Her voice was tight with tension. The dots all joined, and he started to panic.

"Are you alright?"

"I don't have very long. Just a few seconds. I've been kidnapped by a woman. She says you know her."

"Beatrix Rose?"

"Yes," she said. "Beatrix."

Control looked at King and pointed at the phone, mouthing, "It's her."

King picked up his own phone and called the comms room to make sure that the call was being triangulated.

"Daddy?"

"I'm still here."

"She says she wants to talk to you."

"Are you alright . . . ?"

There was no answer, just the sound of the phone being passed.

"Hello, Control."

"Beatrix?"

"Yes."

"If you hurt her . . ."

"What? What are you going to do?"

"I . . ."

"You're not going to do anything apart from what I tell you to do. I don't want to hurt her. If you do what I want, I won't. I won't touch a hair on her head."

He took the phone away from his ear and activated the speaker. "What do you want?"

"To meet. We have a lot to discuss."

"Discuss?"

"In a matter of speaking."

"Are you mad? I know what you've done to the others."

"That's your only choice. You agree to meet me, and I'll bring Cassidy along. As soon as we're done, she's all yours."

King wound his finger in the air, a signal that he should keep her on the phone. Control knew it wouldn't work.

"You'll kill me," he said.

"Want me to send her back to you in pieces?"

Control swallowed. "Where?"

"There's an old drive-in movie theatre outside Carrsville."

"When?"

"Tomorrow morning. Six."

He looked over at King, who nodded at him.

"Alright. We can talk. We can settle this."

"Don't be late."

The line went dead.

Chapter Fifteen

Beatrix had stopped at a grocery store for provisions on the way back from her errands, and Isabella prepared sandwiches for the three of them that evening. She flicked on the TV, and they watched the news and then a sitcom that she hadn't seen before. Cassidy ate sullenly, saying nothing, sitting away from them in a corner of the room. Beatrix had locked the door and was comfortable with her being with them, rather than in the bedroom. The girl had accepted what had happened, and now that there was an end in sight, she seemed willing enough to cooperate.

Beatrix washed up the dirty plates and then cleared the dining table and laid out the items she had purchased at Radio Shack.

She started with the power supply. She cut a metre of intercom wire and stripped the insulation from the ends. She connected one of the ends to a nine-volt battery clip and snapped that onto an AA battery holder. She unscrewed the end of a 1/8" mono plug and connected the stripped wire ends to it, separating each with a piece of electrical tape. The connection looked sound. She slotted the batteries into the holder.

She was aware that Cassidy had turned her attention away from the television and was watching her instead.

"What are you doing?" she asked.

"Never mind."

She put the power supply aside and moved on to the detonator, taking the drill and piercing the plastic casing, making holes for the switch and LED on the front side, and the push button and 1/4" jack on the top. She screwed the components into place and wired them up.

She attached the battery pack and flipped the switch. The LED lit up.

Cassidy was still watching.

"What *is* it?" she asked her more forcefully.

"Watch the TV."

"It's a bomb, isn't it?"

"What it is has nothing to do with you. Just watch the TV."

"This is about my father. You want to kill him."

She felt her anger flicker. "Your father and I have a long history."

"And so you're making a bomb?"

She put the parts down on the table.

"Do you want to know what your father did to me?"

Cassidy said nothing.

"Well? Do you?"

"I won't believe anything you say."

"Did he ever tell you what he did before he came here?"

"He worked for the government."

She chuckled bitterly.

"The civil service," Cassidy added, a moment of confusion on her face.

"How many times have I heard it described like that? He was paid by the government, but not through any budget that ever gets reported."

"What does that mean?"

"Your father was the agent in charge of a team of assassins. Twelve assassins. It was called a lot of things—I've heard the Feathermen, I've heard Echelon, but most of the time it was Group Fifteen. He sent them all around the world. Anyone who was a threat to the interests of the British government, anyone who wouldn't get into line, anyone like that, they were liable to get a visit from one of his agents. I was one of those agents, Cassidy. Your father was my commanding officer."

She laughed at her. "That's crazy."

Beatrix ignored her. "You want to know why I want to speak to your father?" She paused and Cassidy started to interrupt, but Beatrix talked over her. "Ten years ago, your father ordered that two Russian agents in London had to be murdered. We thought it was a standard operation until I found out that he wanted them gone because they were about to expose him as a traitor. And when he found out that I knew what he was doing, he ordered five of my colleagues to murder me and my family."

She paused, and this time Cassidy didn't speak.

"They killed Isabella's father. They shot me. And then, when they found out that I wasn't as easy to kill as they thought I would be, they abducted Isabella and took her away from me. I had to go into hiding until last year. Your father killed my husband. He robbed me of the chance to see my little girl grow up. He took away the only two things I ever cared about."

She pulled up the sleeve of her T-shirt to expose the four roses that had been tattooed onto her right shoulder and arm.

"You see these?"

"Yes," she said quietly.

"Each one is for one of the people who ruined my life. There should be a fifth, but I haven't had time to get that one done yet. There's space for a sixth, too. And that one's for your father."

"You're crazy," she said again, although all the conviction was gone.

"What do you think he's doing in America? What do you *really* think?"

"He's here for work."

"He's here because he's hiding from me. He's been whoring himself to a private security company for years. He thinks that they can protect him. But he's wrong. They can't. No one can. After what he did to me, he might as well have put a gun in his mouth and pulled the trigger. Because no one can stop me, Cassidy. I am relentless. The other five thought that they could hide, but they're all dead. Your father is the last name on my list. And you're going to help me cross him off."

Chapter Sixteen

The apartment that they allotted to Control was a decent size, furnished with the same minimalist zeal that was evident throughout the rest of The Lodge. It was, most importantly, impregnable to everything other than a full-scale infantry assault. It was on the fifth floor of the accommodation block. The lobby was staffed by two armed guards, and there were another half dozen in the barracks connected to the building by a short covered walkway. There was a sniper team on the roof 24/7. The block was at the top of a steep rise, ringed on all sides by a ten-foot fence that was both electrified and topped with razor wire. The forest on all sides had been cleared so that it was impossible to make a covert approach.

It would have made an excellent prison.

Control had conceded that Jamie King had a point, and he had started to carry the Glock that he had provided, even spending time on the range to sharpen up skills that had he had allowed to atrophy over the years through lack of practice.

He had just returned from the range now. He took off the shoulder holster and dropped it and the Glock onto the bed. He took off his shirt and unbuttoned the Kevlar vest that he now wore whenever he was outside. He would have liked to be able to open the window to let the cool air circulate around the room a little, but the windows were bulletproof and sealed shut. The bulletproof glass and the vest were measures that would make it more difficult for Beatrix to go after him with a long gun. Control knew enough of her capabilities to know that those precautions were not superfluous.

He flicked on the TV, gazed morosely at it for a moment and then flicked it off again in favour of the radio. He scrolled through the presets until he found an internet station that was playing "Dark Side of the Moon." He let it play, went into the kitchen and poured himself a glass of wine. He took the glass, returned to the lounge, sat down in the stylish but impractical armchair and thought hard.

Control was a patient man. He had always prided himself on that. He had a temper, a fact to which everyone who had ever worked under him would attest, but that was almost always triggered by incompetence. When a job required a careful approach, he could lie in wait until the right opportunity presented itself.

A man did not last long in his business without endurance and perseverance.

He had gone to war more or less unaware that he had it in him. He had been young and callow, unaware of himself or of what he might go on to achieve. Before he went, those who knew him would have said that he was headstrong and impatient. He came from a background of privilege, a repressed upper-middle-class vacuum that had done nothing to test him, provided no mould into which he could pour his character.

His war had been Ireland. The Troubles had provided incidents that put into doubt his suitability for a career in intelligence. Yet they had also provided others that suggested that, with a little seasoning, he might suit it perfectly. His inexperience was illustrated by his handling of a source who had played him like a cheap fiddle,

using him to lure a patrol into an ambush during which three soldiers were murdered. His ruthlessness, cunning and base instinct
for self-preservation had seen the turncoat assassinated in short
order and the situation dressed up as an intelligence failing from
which he emerged as a hero.

Belfast changed him. It could have broken him, and God
knows, it broke plenty of his colleagues. He saw it every day:
kids like him, fresh out of university and barely ready for their
careers in MI5; experienced soldiers who already had experience
in shooting wars. The battle with the Provos had been a proving
ground. It killed men and ate others up. Control had risen above
it. He had used it. It was the crucible in which his character had
been forged.

He had looked around himself and learned. He had changed
and adapted. He had served in Belfast for four years, and at the
end of it, he had a résumé to be proud of. Some of it was even true.
He had parlayed his record into a posting back home, and then,
when the time had come, he had engineered a transfer into the
department which would become Group Fifteen.

Those early years, he thought while idly listening to the music,
had been the perfect finishing school for the role that he would
eventually fill. He had never seen a dead body before he arrived in
the province. He had never been around death in any capacity. That
double-cross and ambush, and the three dead squaddies, had been
his first experience of bloodshed. He had been the first to find them,
face down, executed with bullets to the back of the head. He had
no idea how he would react before it had happened. He had specu-
lated, considered it empirically from the safety of the sangar, their
fortified position, but there was no substitute for real experience.
Some men would have folded up and broken. Perhaps he would
have been like them?

He wasn't.

His first reaction upon seeing the soldiers in that dingy house on the Falls Road was of curiosity. *This* was what death looked like. It was a thing. A state of being. A simple noun. Something to observe, to analyse, to consider.

His indifference towards it might have been termed callous, or even sadistic, but it was the quality that had made him so resilient over the years. He was a dealer in death. It was his stock-in-trade. There was no room for sadness or regret or any other tawdry emotion that might impede the successful completion of his objectives. He reviewed his targets, planned their ends and then dispatched the men and women who worked as his emissaries, sent them all around the world, carrying with them his orders and the promise of a final exit for those unfortunates whose files had come across his desk.

He had been the head of Group Fifteen for more than a decade. He had outlasted his superiors in MI6, foreign secretaries and prime ministers. He was as resilient as a cockroach. Plenty of files had been passed to him for action during that time. He didn't know exactly how many. He had stopped counting when the count reached four figures.

He thought of his best agents.

John Milton.

Michael Pope.

Beatrix Rose.

His angels of death.

Funny how things changed.

Now he was the hunted.

Not the hunter.

His angels were coming for him.

He got up, walked across to the window and looked out at the desolate swampland beyond the border of the accommodation block.

He saw his reflection in the glass. He looked older now. The grey in his hair was more pronounced, and there was less of it. More wrinkles, etched into the spaces around his eyes. It was worry and fear, carving their marks into his face.

The music played on. He stared out quietly. His eye was drawn to a smudge of black in the air fifty feet away. He focussed on it. It was a Cooper's hawk. He saw its black cap, blue-grey upper parts and white underparts with the distinctive red bars. It was circling on the thermals, a series of lazy loops as it surveyed the terrain below it.

Control exhaled.

His real name was Lucian Finnegan, although no one called him that now. No one had called him that for years. He had been Control for so long that "Lucian" had been subsumed into his new persona, and even he rarely thought of himself that way. His wife called him by his given name, but that had been before they had separated, and they didn't speak now. His children called him "Father."

Maybe he should be Lucian again?

No, he thought. *Lucian is dead. Lucian was Control's first victim.*

He was disturbed by the buzzing of his cellphone. He fished it out of his pocket. It was Jamie King.

"How are you doing?" he asked.

"I've been better."

"I'm sure you have."

"Anything?"

King clucked his tongue in dissatisfaction. "She didn't stay on the call long enough."

"She's no fool. She won't get caught out as easily as that."

"We triangulated to within fifteen miles. She's in the area."

"She's not bluffing, Jamie. She's coming for me."

He watched as the hawk beat its wings, holding position.

"And we're ready for her. It's one woman. I know how good she is. Christ, I've seen what she can do. But it's just one woman, and we have an army. She doesn't have a chance. Not a chance."

The hawk folded back its wings and plunged down to the swamp. It flared at the last moment, exposing its talons, and as it beat the air and began to rise again, he saw something small and helpless writhing in its grip.

He looked away. "What about the rendezvous?"

"It's deserted. Hasn't been used for twenty years. No one goes there anymore. It's not a bad place for her to choose. Good sight lines. Long views. It'll be difficult to surprise her."

"Difficult?"

"I'm working on it. Difficult, not impossible. I've got two fire teams now."

"She'll expect that."

"You'd rather they weren't there?"

"I didn't say that."

"Do you think she's working with anyone else?"

He thought about that. "I wouldn't rule it out. John Milton, perhaps. And he's just as dangerous as she is."

"I don't care how dangerous they are. If she turns up there, she—and anyone else dumb enough to be there with her—is going to be outmatched and outgunned. You have my word on that."

"And my daughter?"

"We'll get her back."

He looked back out of the window and watched as the hawk carried its prey away into the gloom.

"Alright," he said.

"It's nearly over."

"Thanks for calling."

King meant well. He was saying all the things that he was supposed to say, but none of them meant very much. They were not reassuring. It was nearly over, but they did not offer him hope that it would end in his favour. No doubt King meant it. No doubt he was sincere. But he didn't know. He hadn't seen the things that Control had seen.

The oligarch who had barricaded himself inside a fortress and surrounded himself with a private army.

The defector who had retreated to the bosom of the Chinese secret service.

The playboy arms dealer aboard his yacht out at sea, miles from shore.

The government minister in the heart of Baghdad.

Beatrix had passed into their lairs like a spectre.

She had eliminated all of them and dozens more besides.

And she would be waiting for him tomorrow.

One way or another, it was all going to come to an end.

Chapter Seventeen

Beatrix opened the door to the veranda and stepped outside. It was cool and fresh, and the air on her hot and clammy skin was a relief. She knew that she looked wan and frail, and the darkness offered her a chance to hide that, too. She rested her forearms on the balustrade, stared into the black spaces between the trees and then closed her eyes. She was tired.

"Mummy?"

"Hello," she said.

"Are you alright?"

"Yes," Beatrix said. "I'm fine."

"You look . . . you looked . . ."

"Just a little bit tired, Bella," she interrupted gently. "It's alright. I'm fine."

"What are you doing out here?"

"Getting some fresh air."

Isabella was quiet. She settled in next to her mother and nestled close. Beatrix extended her arm to loop it around her shoulders. It was an effort, and she frowned her disquiet at this, wiping the expression away as Isabella tilted her face to look up at her.

"We need to talk about what's going to happen," Beatrix said.

"About what?"

"Tomorrow."

Isabella didn't respond.

"You're going to see things on the news and in the newspapers about me. About what I've done and what I'm going to do. They'll have stories, and those stories won't always be true. Do you understand?"

"Yes. Of course."

"They'll say I was a terrorist. You know what that is, don't you?"

"Yes."

"That's not right. That's not what this is about."

"I know that, Mummy."

She breathed out. "Good girl," she said. "You know I . . . you know . . ."

What was she going to say?

You know I'm doing this for you?

How much of that was true, and how much was the story that she wanted to believe?

How much of it was a self-serving justification for what, she knew, this really was—revenge?

Pure, simple revenge?

She was struck dumb by a moment of confusion.

"They deserved what you've done to them," Isabella said for her. Her tone was clear, certain and confident. "And he deserves it most of all."

Beatrix felt the catch in her throat again. She swallowed it down. "Listen to me," she said. "Whatever happens tomorrow, good or bad, I want you to get straight to the airport. You call Mohammed and you leave."

Isabella looked away.

"I'm serious, sweetheart. You mustn't stay."

"But we said . . ."

She took her daughter's shoulders and held her, facing her square ahead. "I mean it, Isabella."

"But we said, if you can't, if it goes wrong, if it . . ."

"I was wrong about all of that."

"What about my training? That was what it was for. You said: if it goes wrong, I have to finish it. That's my job. That's why I'm here. I take care of all the loose ends."

"No," she said, firmly. "That was wrong. I was wrong."

"So what was it all for if it wasn't for this?"

"I was wrong, Bella. This has nothing to do with you. It's my fight. It always has been my fight, and I should never have involved you. Your training is for you to defend yourself, if that's ever necessary. It isn't for this." She waved her hand at the darkness, meaning it to encompass Control and Manage Risk and what she had resolved to do. "As soon as it's over, I want you to get away, as far as you can, whatever happens."

Her daughter frowned.

"Do you understand, Bella?"

She didn't look at her. "Yes."

"*Isabella?*"

"I understand."

"Good girl."

"Now," she said, changing the subject to the other thing for which she needed reassurance. "You know about the money?"

"Yes," Isabella said. "I remember."

"It's in your name. All you'll have to do is visit the bank with your passport, and they'll give you access to it."

"I know, Mummy."

"There's a lot. A million. More than you'll need."

"I know," she said. "I know all of this."

"I just want to make sure. I'll sleep easier."

They stayed out on the veranda, quiet with their thoughts. Beatrix hugged her daughter close to her, feeling her warmth against her flank, smelling the citrus notes from the shampoo that they had found in the cabin's bathroom. She closed her eyes, and soon the sound of the television that Cassidy was watching inside was lost to her, and all she could hear was the chirping of crickets and the rustle of the breeze as it stirred the leaves and branches all around them.

They stood there, peaceful and calm, and she allowed herself to imagine another life, a different one, one in which there was no cancer, no revenge. One in which there was a future. The thought of it, so tantalising, seemed almost real, and she hugged Isabella closer. A spasm of pain flickered like summer lightning along her nerves and into her synapses: a glimpse, a little reminder, that her dreams were mirages, siren songs that would lead her to her doom if she paid them any heed. Reality crashed down, weakness and pain and the sure promise of the end, and she had to bite her lip to stifle her sob.

Isabella knew. She slipped her arm around her mother's waist and squeezed gently. She laid her head on her shoulder, and Beatrix could do nothing to staunch her tears.

———

She didn't sleep that night. She knew it would be impossible, and so she didn't try. The pain was constant now, and there was nothing she could do to alleviate it. She had grown used to it. It helped to keep in mind the fact that it would all be ending soon enough. One way or another, it would come to an end. She stayed in the sitting room, huddled in the glow of a small standard lamp and warmed by the logs she tossed onto the fire.

She thought about her life and the things that she had achieved.

She addressed her regrets and acknowledged the things that she would have done differently.

She thought of Lucas, her husband. He had been South African, had installed high-end AV systems, and he had been her opposite. Where she was fiery and impetuous, he had been calm and dependable, with soulful brown eyes that shone with patience and compassion. She knew very well that she had been difficult in the early years of their marriage, that she had put her career first and that, when she was at home, she had been prey to quicksilver mood swings that were triggered by the frustration that other agents were in the field, living the life, when she was not. She had been selfish. She had lied to him about what she did, and even though she knew that he was too wise to be fooled, he had never pressed. She thought of the weeks she spent abroad and how she would close herself off to him when she returned home. She had failed in her vows, and yet he had always stood by her and she had never been in any doubt that he loved her.

She remembered the look he had given her before Lydia Chisholm had shot him.

It's alright. I understand. I sacrifice myself for my daughter and my wife, and I do it gladly.

———⌣———

She thought of the day that Isabella was born. She had been given extended leave (although she had only intended to take six weeks before she reported back for duty), and she and Lucas had camped out at their home in London's East End. The pregnancy had seemed to take an eternity, and when Isabella had been a few days late, she had been anxious to move things along. They had gone for a walk in the local park. She remembered the reds and oranges and the smell of freshness undercut with damp and rot that presaged the change from late summer to autumn. She remembered the cramps that she had dismissed as false labour and then the sudden crescendo, the call for an ambulance that had arrived too late, and Lucas, calm despite it all, delivering their daughter, holding her in his hands, with a look of happy disbelief at this thing that they had done.

She thought about the invitation to join Group Fifteen. That had been the pivot about which everything else had turned. Control had delivered the offer himself. He had been different then, or at least she remembered him differently. He was persuasive in the way that public schoolboys often are, a mixture of unshakeable confidence, innate bravado and the sense that an offer like this, when delivered by someone like him, was impossible to reject by someone like her.

And perhaps that was right. Perhaps it was impossible.

She could remember the smallest details of that day. She had returned to the barracks after a difficult patrol, and he had been there waiting for her. He had been wearing a blue-and-white-striped shirt and a suit despite the baking heat. His skin was fresh and bright, as rosy red and waxy as an apple, and he was wearing the same cologne that she would remember for the rest of her life, the scent that would haunt her darkest hours, instantly evocative, sometimes as strong as the smell of the opium she would eventually inhale to forget it.

She had been younger then, with fewer responsibilities. The chance to join an elite team, off the books, with carte blanche to operate anywhere in the world, was intoxicating. She had grown up on the novels of Fleming and Le Carré, and here was her chance to inhabit those worlds herself.

How could she have refused him?

She could not.

But she wished, *how* she wished, that she had.

She opened her eyes.

It was quiet. The only noises were the crackle of the flames and the sound of deep, relaxed breathing from the bedroom.

Isabella.

She remembered when she had been taken from her. The terror on her face. She had been three years old, barely more than a baby, and she had been next to her father as he had been shot. She had watched as her mother had ignored a bullet to the shoulder and stabbed a woman in the throat. Death and blood and then her mother abandoning her to strangers. How much of that did she remember? How had it changed her? Her innocence had been polluted that afternoon. The years that followed had tarnished it more, and then, despite all of her best intentions, Beatrix feared that the year they had spent together had destroyed whatever was left.

Had there been a choice?

Isabella would be on her own soon, and the world was a cruel and unkind place.

She had needed to prepare her for it.

─── ───

Beatrix crept into the bedroom at five in the morning. It was still dark outside, the first light of dawn just starting to silver the horizon at the far reaches of the lake. She touched Isabella on the shoulder, and when she stirred, she gestured that she should come into the sitting room.

Beatrix waited for her there.

"I've got to go now," she said. "It's time."

Isabella didn't reply.

"We've nearly done it now. Everything that needs to be done. It's close."

Isabella's composure cracked as she tried to choke back a sob.

"You understand, don't you, Bella?"

She nodded as tears slicked her cheeks.

Beatrix felt as if her heart was being torn into a million tiny pieces.

Isabella looked up at her through eyes filmed with tears. "Can't you do it tomorrow?"

"No, Bella, it has to be today. You know it does."

She looked at her with a heartbreaking clarity in her wet eyes. "Because you're ill?"

"Yes," she said. "I'm weak. I don't know how much longer I'll be able to do what I need to do. I don't have very long left."

Isabella wiped the back of her hand across her eyes and took a steadying breath. "I know you have to do it. I understand."

She told her what she would have to do next. She would have to stay with Cassidy for the rest of the day, and then she would leave her, still tied to the bed, and hike up to the main road. She would call a taxi from there and then head back to Philadelphia. She had plenty of money, and Beatrix had already bought a ticket to take her back to Paris. She would call Mohammed from the airport, and Mohammed would meet her at Charles de Gaulle. "You'll live with him and Fatima from now on. They'll look after you."

Isabella sobbed, choking it back again.

"Ignore what they say about me."

"Yes."

"And you mustn't stay. No matter what."

Isabella hugged her, arms around her chest, squeezing her tight. Beatrix dipped her head to her daughter's shoulder and buried her face in her blonde hair. She filled her nostrils with her scent and promised herself that she would remember it for the few hours she had left.

Isabella's eyes were streaming with tears. "I love you, Mummy."

"I love you too, Bella."

She disengaged herself. She was crying now—there was no point in trying to stop it—and she turned and walked away to the car. She got in, biting her lip so hard that she tasted her own blood, the taste of copper, like old pennies, and she wiped her face on her sleeve.

She turned the ignition and pulled away.

She had been dealt a bad hand, the worst hand, and this was the only way that she knew to play it. Isabella wouldn't be safe if she lost her nerve. Her own death was a certainty, anyway. It couldn't be avoided; it could only be deferred. She would end her life at a time of her choosing and, in the flames of her death, she would ensure her daughter's future.

That was a trade worth making.

She would make that trade any day.

And that would be her legacy.

She dared not turn back, but she glanced into the mirror. Isabella was waiting on the veranda, watching, and she hadn't moved as Beatrix turned the car into the gentle corner and finally put her out of sight.

She drove on to Suffolk, eventually stopping on a side road where she was sure she was out of sight. She opened the trunk and poured the first two bottles of the nitromethane into the first tub of petrol and the other two into the second.

The unfinished detonator was in the trunk, too. She took the nichrome wire and wrapped it around the casing, fastening alligator clips to the stripped wire and connecting them to the power supply. She left the detonator in the trunk and unrolled the wire so that it reached through to the front of the car. She plugged the 1/8" plug into the power supply, switched the toggle across so that it was unarmed, plugged in the battery, armed it and pushed the button. It worked. She switched it off, switched the toggle across so that the detonator was armed and rested it on the seat next to her.

She put the car into gear and drove on. The sun was rising over the tops of the trees. She needed to hurry.

Chapter Eighteen

Cassidy was sitting on the bed, her back pressed up against the headboard. Isabella was sitting diagonally opposite her, able to see the door, the window and the girl without shifting in the seat. The little Beretta was in her lap, her fingers resting across it. They had been in the same position for two hours.

"This is bullshit," Cassidy said. She started to stand.

"Don't," Isabella warned, slipping her index finger through the trigger finger.

"Why are you doing this?"

"I'm not going to talk to you," Isabella said. "I told you."

"I mean, come on, how old are you? Fifteen?"

She didn't answer.

"Seriously? Younger than that? Fourteen?"

"I'm not . . ."

"*Thirteen?* Jesus. You're thirteen years old, and you're pointing a gun at me? How fucked up is that?"

Isabella glared at her.

"You should be in school or something, right?"

She didn't respond.

"You're just going to sit there staring at me while your fucked-up mother tries to kill my father? You know what that means, right? It *is* clear to you? That makes you an accessory. To murder. You're going to go to prison."

"It won't be anything I haven't done already," she said quietly.

"What?"

Isabella shook her head. She wasn't going to be drawn into a conversation with her. Her mother had warned against that. The distraction, taking your eye off the ball—that was what she had told her. She had to focus.

Cassidy scowled angrily, and then, before Isabella could say anything, she stood.

"*Fuck* this shit."

Isabella stood, too, aimed the gun, gestured with her other hand for her to sit. "Back down."

"What are you going to do?"

"I'll shoot you."

"No, you won't."

"I'll shoot you in the knee." She lowered her aim. "You want to be able to dance after this, don't you? How are you going to dance with a smashed-up knee? Don't think I won't."

Cassidy looked at her, and for a moment, Isabella thought that she was going to call her bluff. She sighed and shook her head and sat back down again.

They settled back into the same pattern for the next half an hour. Cassidy turned on the bedroom TV, flicking through the TV channels with surly stabs of her finger, and sighed unhappily.

She settled on an episode of *Malcolm in the Middle*.

The episode finished and Cassidy stood again.

"Sit down," Isabella said.

"No, seriously, this isn't any good. I need the bathroom."

Isabella frowned.

"What? I can't go to the bathroom? What do you want me to do?"

"That's fine. You can go. But I have to come with you."

"You want to come in? Fine. Whatever."

Isabella approached her cautiously and unknotted the rope. Cassidy went around the bed to the bathroom and undid her belt. "So you're coming in then?"

Isabella relented. "It's alright. I can see you from here."

She looked down at the gun in her hand as Cassidy sat down on the toilet. She felt the catch in her throat as she thought about her mother. There was a pain in her chest. An ache. She knew she wouldn't see her again. Isabella was too observant to miss how ill she had become and how quickly it had overtaken her. She had known for weeks, from the way that Mohammed and her mother would stop talking when she came into the room, to the bottle of pills that she found on the dining room table when her mother had forgotten to take them with her. The internet had told her all she needed to know about them.

She knew she was going to lose her mother, so soon after she had found her again, and she didn't know how she was going to cope. She had spent so long holding her feelings to herself, compressing her hopes and fears into tiny packages that she could secret away from the foster parents that had come and gone throughout the unhappy years of her childhood that she didn't know whether she would be able to find the words to express the way that she felt. She didn't know to whom she would express herself, either. There would be Mohammed and Fatima, she supposed, but they were thousands of miles away. She was in a country that she didn't know, and she knew, because her mother had told her, a lot of people would be looking for her very soon.

She was still staring at the gun, her vision unfocussed, when the door to the bathroom slammed shut.

Her focus snapped right back, and she pushed herself off the bed.

She heard the click of the lock.

"Open the door!"

She heard the sound of frantic activity inside the bathroom.

She tried the handle, but the lock held firm. She drove her shoulder at it, but her willowy frame was much too light to shift it.

There was a bang, and then another.

"I'll shoot it open!"

Isabella raised the gun and pointed it at the handle. Her aim wavered, uncertainly.

There was a bang and then the sound that a sticky window might make as it was thumped open.

Oh no.

The window.

At the back.

She ran to the other side of the room and unlocked the front door, throwing it open to the cool day outside. She scrambled around to the back of the cabin, and there it was—the window, wide open. She turned to the undergrowth and thought she saw a flash of motion, squinted into the light at it, but then it was gone.

She froze.

The world was spread out before her, with its innumerable options, but it stopped her cold. She waited there, fumbling the gun beneath the folds of her jumper, uncertain of what her mother would want her to do and crippled by her uncertainty.

She had failed.

She had let her down.

She ran back into the cabin again, took her bag and swept in her little purse, the money, her phone and the other bits and pieces that she had taken out during their stay. She saw Cassidy's leather jacket and took that, too. She took the handles of her mother's bag, lifting that with her own, and rushed back across the room. She pushed the little gun into her pocket and hurried outside.

Chapter Nineteen

Beatrix pulled off the road and rolled up to the entrance to the abandoned drive-in. It was a large, wide space, with the stained old screen faced by broad rows that were set aside for parking. Each bay was furnished with a metal post from which the speakers would once have hung. Some were still there, dangling from their wires, swinging to and fro in the light breeze. The area was encircled by a wire mesh fence, and signs fixed onto it by local realtors indicated that it was available for redevelopment. Beatrix revved the engine. There was a wooden shack ahead of her and the remains of the entrance barrier. The wooden arm had been broken off, and it lay impotently at the side of the road. She let out the brake and edged ahead.

There were speed bumps every ten metres, and every fresh jolt sent a spasm of pain through her body. She felt terribly, awfully weak, as if every last scrap of humanity had been sucked out of her. It was as bad as she had ever felt. If any kind of physical exertion was necessary today, then she was finished. She knew she would be as helpless as a baby. Her arms felt like lead weights, and it was as much as she could manage to turn the wheel. Her fingers held onto it like claws.

The access road encircled the main parking area, and it was necessary to circle around it to reach the secondary entrance. She edged around the road, looking out for any sign that she was driving into an ambush.

———

The first sniper team was designated Hawk. They were established on the eastern side of the drive-in. The lot was set in a shallow bowl, its raised edges covered in overgrown scrub and unhealthy-looking shrubs and small trees. They had found a good spot while it was still dark. They were wearing ghillie suits, camouflaged expertly so that they practically merged into the vegetation.

The car peeled off the main road and slowed as it approached the entrance to the drive-in. Scraps of discarded newsprint caught in the breeze, plastered up against the mesh fence.

"Call it out," the sniper said to his spotter.

The second man held his binoculars to his eyes.

"Target. Sector Alpha. Deep. Vehicle. Looks like an Impala."

"Range it."

"Four hundred yards and closing. Wind, one-half value, push one left."

"Passengers?"

"Negative. Just the driver."

"On target. Call it in."

The spotter opened the channel. "Command post, command post, this is Hawk, over."

"We copy your traffic, Hawk. What have you got?"

"Visual confirmation of target's current position."

The radio crackled again as the second sniper team reported in. "Command post, this is Eagle, over."

"Copy that, Eagle. Proceed."

"Also confirming eyes on target. She's just inside the perimeter. Only the driver is visible. Repeat, package is not visible in the car."

"Copy that. Hawk and Eagle, hold position. Fire only on my command."

———

The formation of helicopters swooped low and fast, the long muddy expanse of the Great Dismal Swamp just fifty feet below. Control was in the trailing chopper, a MH-6J. It was a fast two-man ship, used by the Border Patrol down south, and used by Manage Risk to ferry key staff around their vast facility. The second bird, an AH-64 Apache, was a twin-engine attack chopper that bristled with weapons. The company had purchased six of them from Boeing at a combined cost of $100 million. They were brought out only for special occasions, and this was one of them.

Control was not about to underestimate what Beatrix Rose was capable of, and Jamie King was prepared to back his assessment all the way.

The cabin was compact, and Control was not particularly comfortable. The body armour jagged into his ribs and prodded into his soft flesh whenever he so much as flinched.

He could live with the discomfort when it might be the difference between life and death.

They flew west. Cars headed north and south, into and out of Suffolk, and Control looked down on them with envy. People going about their daily lives. Dreary, early commutes into the office. All of that was very attractive to him now. He would gladly have exchanged his life for one on predictable mundanity. He knew exactly what he was flying into. It felt like he was voluntarily putting his neck in the guillotine.

The drive-in appeared in the near distance.

Control watched with avid, almost manic, interest as his pilot turned through sixty degrees and followed the line of the main road until they reached the access road.

"Looks like she's here before us," the pilot said, pointing to the car in the middle of the lot.

He took up a pair of high-powered field glasses and examined the car as the pilot pulled up the nose and slowed. Beatrix Rose was sitting in the front seat. It looked as if she was alone. The car was parked to face the big, dirty wooden screen that would once have been wrapped with canvas. It was almost as if she had arrived to watch a film that would never be shown.

"Chalk One to Command Post," Control said into his headset microphone.

"Copy that. Go ahead, Chalk One."

"Run a license check on plate number ADC-143."

"Copy that. Stand by."

He was terrified, and it was difficult to hide it. There was fear for his daughter, of course, but mostly it was fear for himself. He knew what Beatrix wanted. It was obvious. She hadn't kidnapped Cassidy to bring him out here for a face-to-face. They had nothing to talk about. She had made that abundantly plain with the executions of the five agents.

The agents who had let him down. He had no pity for them. They had reaped what they had sown. It was their own negligent failures that had sealed their death warrants.

He *knew* what Rose wanted.

"Command post to Chalk One. Come in, over."

"Go ahead."

"The car is registered to an address in New Jersey. It was stolen a year ago."

Control absorbed the information and processed it, but didn't respond.

Beatrix was sitting in the front seat, her hands resting on the wheel. No sign of any weapons, but she had to be armed. She was as still as a statue. As the chopper edged around to face the car, he saw her clearly, staring impassively up at it. The cockpit windshield was tinted, and she couldn't possibly have seen him, but he felt as if she could. He felt as if she was staring right through it and right at him.

"Command post to Chalk One. Copy?"

He couldn't see the snipers, but he knew that they were there.

Both teams would have her zeroed.

All he had to do was give the word, and she would cease to be a problem.

But what about Cassidy?

His daughter was the only thing that stayed his hand.

"Command Post to Chalk . . ."

"Find out where that fucking car has been."

"We're trying, sir."

Beatrix sat back in the seat and watched as the two helicopters circled her like raptors waiting to pounce down upon their prey. They called the MH-6J the Little Bird. She guessed that he was inside it. The bird had no armour and was probably within range of the explosion that she could trigger in a heartbeat. She had it within her power to bring all of this to an end, right here and now, but she did not. She needed more. She needed to see his face again before she scraped him off the face of the earth.

She knew, of course, that they were not alone. The first sniper was well hidden, but she had known where to look. There was a two-man team on the lip of the bowl, reasonably well obscured with ghillie suits, but facing into the sun. She had seen the glint of daylight on the spotter's binoculars.

The second team was almost adjacent to the first, on the other side of the bowl.

There was nowhere for her to hide. She could slip down beneath the wheel, but she was willing to bet that both soldiers were equipped with .50 calibre rifles, and bullets as big as that would cut through the bodywork like a hot knife through butter. The two of them had her in the middle of a killing zone that she wouldn't be able to escape from.

But she was alright with that.

She didn't want to escape.

She reached into her shirt and took out her locket. She opened it and looked down at the picture of Isabella as a baby.

The Apache circled out from behind the MH-6J, providing its weapons with a clear line of fire.

She woke up her cellphone in its dashboard mount and called the number for Control.

"Beatrix," his voice played out of the speaker.

"I told you not to bring anyone," she said, "and you've brought a party."

"You didn't expect . . ."

"I expected you to care a little bit more about what might happen to your daughter."

"Where is she?"

"Not far."

"Is she with John Milton?"

"You don't need to worry about that."

"If you've hurt her . . ."

"You're not in a position to make threats, Control."

"Neither are you."

Yes, I am, she thought. *I have nothing to lose.*

"Where is she?"

She didn't reply. She could almost sense his anger and frustration.

"Beatrix?"

"She won't be hurt if you do exactly what I tell you to do."

"What do you want?"

"I want you to land."

She looked up at the Little Bird and then across to the Apache. The snipers seemed redundant now. The Apache had a full combat load: the big, brutal 30mm chain gun between the main landing gear, four hard points on the stub wings that were laden with Hellfire missiles and Hydra rocket pods.

She felt the hard shape of the trigger clutched in her fist. It was a dead man's switch. If she was shot, her hand would spasm and her grip would be released. The relay would be complete, and the bomb would detonate.

"Bring that bird down, Control. Right now."

The Little Bird descended, the pilot landing deftly a hundred feet away.

"Be ready to take off," he said to the pilot.

"Yes, sir."

He nodded up at the Apache. "Tell them to wait for my signal."

"Yes, sir. They know."

"When I'm ready, I want her wiped off the face of the planet."

He took a deep breath. His knees felt like water.

Come on. See it through.

He opened the cabin door and pushed it back against the fuselage, the downdraft from the blades wrapping him in a vortex of cold air. He stepped down, holding onto the edge of the door for support, and then set off towards the Impala.

He heard the sound of Beatrix's voice in the Bluetooth buds that were pressed into his ears. "That's better. Come over to me."

His phone buzzed with another call.

He pulled the phone out of his pocket and looked at the display.

He didn't recognise the number. He cancelled the call.

He looked up at the car.

Beatrix gestured for him to come ahead to her.

The phone buzzed again.

He stared at the number.

The Apache hovered menacingly.

He looked back at Beatrix.

She opened the door and stepped outside.

The phone buzzed. He cancelled it again.

The driver's door opened, and Beatrix stepped out of the car. The downdraft from the two choppers tousled her blonde hair and tugged at her clothes. Control was shocked. She was emaciated, and she moved with difficulty and evident pain, as if she had aged fifty years in the decade since he had seen her last. She looked feeble. He looked at her, and he couldn't believe that she had dispatched five of his best operatives.

The phone buzzed again.

He selected the new call and put the phone to his ear.

"*What?*"

"Daddy!"

"Cassidy?"

"I'm fine."

He took a step back.

"Where are you?"

Frustration flicked across Beatrix's face.

"I got away. I'm fine."

"Where . . ."

"It's a trap, Daddy. She's got a bomb."

Beatrix saw the change of expression on Control's face and knew the game was up.

He turned away from her, stumbling, and then jerked his arm in her direction. "Shoot her!" he yelled over the noise of the rotors as he started to run.

The chain gun whirled and whirred as it spooled up.

A double track of bullets started to chew up the asphalt, racing towards her.

She gripped the locket in her left hand.

She released her grip on the trigger with her right.

The electrical relay completed and current passed through it.

Thoughts raced through her mind in a last mad, crazy tangle without form or structure.

Isabella.

Mohammed.

Fatima.

John Milton.

Michael Pope.

Control.

Dear Lucas.

The scene in her front room, ten years ago, a different world.

Spenser.

Chisholm.

Joyce.

Duffy.

English.

Control.

Her cancer.

Isabella.

Isabella.

The trigger passed the signal to the detonator, the circuit was completed and the explosive charge ignited a fraction of a fraction of a second before the petrol and the fertiliser in the trunk erupted. The firestorm blew the Impala into a billion tiny pieces and swept out in a monstrous, savage, cleansing wave.

Chapter Twenty

Isabella had hiked back through the undergrowth until she could see the freeway again. She moved slowly and carefully, acutely aware that Cassidy would contact the police and that their first move would be to hurry to the cabin where they had been staying. She had to keep out of sight. Her caution meant that it took her over an hour to reach the road, and she followed it inside the wooded margins for another hour until she was confident that she was far enough from the cabin to hitch a ride into town.

She had had to wait only ten minutes before a car pulled over and the driver leaned over to open the passenger side door.

"Where you headed?" the driver said.

"Chesapeake."

"Me too. Hop in."

She did, assessing him quickly as she slipped in beside him. He was in his late middle age, dressed in a cheap suit and a white shirt with a dirty collar. He smelled a little, as if he hadn't showered for a few days, and the back seat was strewn with clothes, empty fast food packaging and Styrofoam cups.

"What you doing out here on your own?" he said as they pulled into the light early morning traffic.

"I've been hiking," she said.

He looked over at her. "Really?" He smiled, revealing small and yellowed teeth. "At seven in the morning?"

"Yes," she said.

"You aren't dressed for it."

"I'm headed back into town," she said hurriedly, her story already falling apart. "I was camping with some friends. We argued and so I left."

He looked across at her, still smiling. "How old are you?"

She felt vulnerable, stuck in a car with a man she didn't know. Her bag was open at the end farthest away from the man, and she slipped her hand inside, her fingers bumping up against the cold metal of the little pistol.

"How old are you, sugar?" he asked again.

"I'm thirteen."

"And your friends? How old are they?"

"Older."

"And they let you just walk away?"

"That's right."

"You want maybe I should call the police? I don't know much about the criminal law or nothing like that, but, you ask me, that's child neglect or some such thing."

"It's alright," she said. "I'd rather just speak to my mother about it."

"Where are you from?"

"What do you mean?"

"Your accent. You're not local, are you?"

"Oh," she said. "No. I'm not. I'm English. I live with my father most of the time, outside London. My parents are divorced."

"Oh, I . . ."

She smiled awkwardly at his embarrassment. "My mother lives here, though. Chesapeake. I visit her twice a year."

"And you've got friends who let you wander off in the middle of nowhere?"

"Cousins, actually."

"Mm-hmm."

He was quiet for a moment, staring out at the sparse lines of traffic, but she could see that he was processing all the answers she had given him. He didn't strike her as very smart, but he wouldn't need to be to realise that she was full of it, and every answer she gave surely made it more and more obvious.

She could feel the cold steel of the pistol beneath her fingertips.

The police would be looking for her as soon as they had pieced together what had happened. There would be an appeal when they couldn't find her, maybe something on the television. This man, if he watched it, would remember her very well indeed.

She had already drawn enough attention to herself.

What would her mother have said?

Would she have been disappointed?

What would she have done?

She changed her plan. She had to get out.

They were on the edge of Chesapeake and fast approaching a gas station surrounded by collection of fast food restaurants.

"Here, please," she said. "This is fine."

"You don't want me to take you into town?"

"No, really. This is fine. My mother can get me from here."

"Fair enough." He flicked the indicator and turned onto the exit ramp.

There was a parking lot behind the gas station and the restaurants, and he pulled up into an empty space.

"I kind of think I should stay and say something to your mother. I don't know—it's not right you being left out on the road like that, so young and all."

"That's alright," she said, quickly opening the door.

She got out and closed the door.

He leaned over and rolled the window down.

"You sure you're alright?"

"Yes," she said, gripping the straps of the bag. "Thank you."

He watched her for a moment, and then, with a shrug, rolled the window back up, reversed and headed back onto the ramp to merge with the flow of traffic.

Isabella ground her teeth. That had been a mistake. Badly handled. She needed to do better.

She hefted the bag and walked to the restaurants.

The waitress watched the young girl as she sat at the table. She was staring at the news on the TV.

She took her notepad from the pouch in the front of her apron and went over to her.

"Morning, honey. How are you today?"

"I'm fine," the girl said, her eyes still on the TV.

"What can I get you?"

She glanced quickly down at the menu, said, "Pancakes, please, and a glass of orange juice," and then looked back to the screen.

"Coming right up."

The waitress went back to the kitchen and relayed the order. Five minutes later, she collected the plate and the juice and took them over to the girl's table.

"Here you go, darling."

"Thank you."

There was something strange about the girl, and the waitress was musing on that as she went to take the order from a family who had settled at a table on the other side of the restaurant. When she had finished with them, she looked back at the girl again. She was still staring up at the screen, a faraway look on her face. She hadn't touched the pancakes or the juice.

The waitress returned to her table again. "Are you alright, honey?"

The girl looked up her. Her eyes were the clearest blue, almost translucent, and the effect of her stare was disconcerting.

"Pardon me?"

"The pancakes alright? You haven't touched them. Can I get you something else?"

"Oh no," she said, distractedly. "They'll be fine."

The girl's eyes went back to the screen.

The waitress turned to look. It was a news special, an outside broadcast. There had been some sort of explosion. She watched the report for a moment before she recognised the old drive-in movie theatre out at Carrsville. The blackened wreckage of a car was visible in the big parking lot in the distance, over the shoulder of the reporter. There was a helicopter, too, a little one that looked as if it had crashed. It had fallen onto its side. The entrance to the drive-in had been cordoned off with black and yellow crime scene tape that twitched in the wind. A number of police vehicles, their lights flashing, were parked on the perimeter.

"Hey, Herb," she called out to the short-order cook, "Turn up the TV, will you?"

Herb aimed the remote in the vague direction of the old set and enabled the volume. The reporter, a local whom the waitress recognised from years of watching the same channel, was interviewing a man identified as the chief of police.

"So what are you saying?" the man asked. "You're saying it was a bomb?"

"I have to qualify all this by saying the investigation is in its early stages, but, yes, that's what it looks like. A car bomb. Now, if you're asking me who was responsible for this, that I can't say, not right now."

"But you think it's terrorism?"

"That's a possibility we're looking into."

"Are there any victims?"

"Yes," he said. "One fatality."

"Do you have any details?"

"We think it's a woman."

"And any injuries?"

"Yes, one man, very badly burnt. He's been taken to Norfolk General in Ghent. More than that, I can't say right now. I'd just be speculating."

The waitress looked back at the girl. She had turned from the screen and was eating, staring at her plate, deliberately slicing the pancakes into neat squares. She dabbed each portion in maple syrup and then put it in her mouth.

She wore a determined and serious frown.

———

Isabella paid for her breakfast and went to the pay phone in the lobby of the restaurant. There was a stack of business cards for taxi firms on the little shelf below the telephone, and she flipped through them until she found one that she liked. She called the number and ordered a car. There was a Yellow Pages on the shelf, and she turned the pages to H and then "Hotels." She tore the page out, folding it into a neat square and sliding it into her pocket.

She waited outside in the cold sunlight until the car arrived.

"Where to, honey?"

"The Greenbrier Mall, please."

"Sure thing."

She sat in the back. The driver made no attempt to start a conversation; that was a relief. She unzipped the bag and, careful not to give herself away, reached inside and riffled through the thick wad of bank notes. There were fifties and hundreds there, a big stack of them. That was good. She was going to need money. She peeled off a fifty for the cab, keeping that in her hand, and then five hundreds for the hotel. She took out an additional three hundred, put the notes in her pocket and zipped the bag shut again.

She stared with glazed eyes at the warehouses and strip malls on the edge of the city, thinking of the pictures that she had seen on the television in the restaurant. The car was just a blackened shell, but enough of it remained for her to recognise it as the car that her mother had driven to bring them to Chesapeake.

The policeman had said that there had been one victim.

A woman.

Isabella's bottom lip began to quiver. She bit it, determined not to cry in the taxi. That would lead to more questions. It would make her stand out in the driver's memory. She couldn't afford that. She needed to be anonymous. There would be time for tears later.

She composed herself, and the moment passed.

The reporter had said that a man had been injured and was being treated in hospital.

He had said that the hospital was in Ghent.

She would have to find out where that was.

─── ───

She had the taxi drop her off in the centre of the mall so that she could buy the things that she would need before she went to the hotel. The place was as big as a football stadium, a sprawling two-storey monster that stood in the middle of a vast parking lot, orbited by its own access road. The taxi rumbled across the empty space and parked next to the entrance to Macy's. Isabella paid, thanked the driver and stepped outside. There was a wide door, lots of chrome and glass, and she walked over to it and pushed her way inside.

The door led straight into the perfume section. The air was heavy with dizzying scent. She walked between the tables and counters laden with expensive products, the attendants made up as flawlessly as air hostesses, until she was in the main thoroughfare that ran through the centre of the mall. There were dozens of shops and outlets. The noise of the shoppers echoed off the shiny floors, all scrubbed clean, and produced a hubbub that Isabella found a little disorientating. The past year in Marrakech had inured her to noise and clamour, but this was different. The souk was chaotic and vital, but this was bloodless and corporate, a thousand people circulating with vacant eyes. Insipid music played over the PA system. Isabella had been to malls during her childhood in England, but they were smaller and more tawdry than this. She'd never experienced anything quite like it, and she found it unsettling.

She walked on until she found a branch of T-Mobile. There were dozens of cellphones on display, all fixed to the wall, with cards extolling their various virtues. She went inside and made her way to the nearest display.

An assistant detached himself from his station and glided over to her.

"Can I help you?"

"Yes," she said. "I'm looking for a phone."

"I can help you with that." He brightened with interest as he smelt the possibility of an easy upsell and a bigger commission. "What would you mostly be using it for?"

"Making calls and browsing the internet."

"And do you have a budget?"

She thought of the bundle of notes in her bag. "Two hundred dollars?"

The assistant reached up to the display and took down a Samsung handset. "This is the Galaxy Light," he said before launching into an explanation of its features that he recited as if he had learned it by rote. Isabella tuned out and thought about the other things that she was going to have to do before she was ready.

"I'll take it," she said when he was done.

She followed him to the back of the shop and filled out the paperwork. It was a prepaid phone, and since she paid cash, there wasn't even a need to give her name. It came with a limited amount of airtime and data, and she bought an upgrade to boost those up to a level she was more comfortable with.

She thanked the assistant and went outside again.

There was a pharmacy next door, and she stopped there to buy a packet of hair dye and a jar of Vaseline.

It was two miles north to the hotel that she had selected. The town seemed like it was a pleasant place, with lots of broad and well-trimmed lawns on either side of the road and a host of shopping outlets. The taxi followed Greenbrier Parkway over the Hampton Roads Beltway until it reached Woodlake Drive.

The Staybridge Suites were found within two matching five-storey apartment blocks surrounded by well-tended gardens. According to the section of the Yellow Pages she had ripped from the book, the apartments could be taken for short- or long-term stays. The area was away from the middle of town and looked private and discreet. It looked anonymous, the kind of place where people would drift in and out without leaving a ripple. That was important.

She took a deep breath, pushed open the door and approached the desk.

The clerk was a middle-aged woman with a friendly face. "Hello, sweetheart" she said. "How are you doing today?"

"I'm very well, thank you."

"What can I do for you?"

"I'd like a room, please."

"Would you, now. How old are you?"

"Sixteen."

"Really? You look younger than that."

"No, I am," she said, taking out her fake passport. "Look."

She placed it on the desk, open to the page with her picture and details. The clerk put on a pair of glasses and studied it, comparing the picture with her face. "Sixteen," she said. "Goodness me. You look so much younger than that."

"Do you have any rooms?"

"Are you travelling on your own, sweetie?"

"I'm with my father. He's meeting someone in town. He's on business."

"Is he in the military?"

"That's right," she said.

The woman nodded. "Most of our guests are. What is it? Lockheed Martin? Raytheon?"

"Northrop Grumman," she said, reciting the information she had read in the hotel's ad.

"Northrop? We got some others working over there in at the moment. Some conference or other."

"That's right. That's why he's here."

"Well then, let's get you registered." The woman tapped a key on her keyboard and consulted her screen. "A room," she said. "Yes, we do have a room. You want one for both of you? A twin?"

"Yes, please. For a week."

"Alright, then. I'll need a credit card."

"I can pay now," she said. "My father prefers cash. Is that alright?"

"Sure."

The room cost five hundred dollars for the week. Isabella took out the money and handed it over. The clerk put the notes in the till, printed out the details of the booking and slipped two keycards into a small paper wallet. She gave it to Isabella and told her that the room was on the third floor of the building they were in.

"Thank you," she said.

———

The room was simple and clean. She only planned to stay in it for a few days, and it would serve her very well for what she needed. She used the clear plastic wand to close the blinds and locked the door. She ordered a takeout delivery, and after she had eaten, she spent a couple of hours with the smartphone, logging onto the hotel's WiFi so that she could monitor the news. The police had little to add to the initial reports of the explosion. They confirmed that the victim was connected to Manage Risk, the security company headquartered in the area, and, as such, they said that terrorism was now considered to be the most likely motive. The bomber had been so thoroughly immolated in the blast that identification was proving difficult. All they knew was that it was a woman.

She switched on the television and left it on in the background. There were regular bulletins, and she focussed her attention on the screen for those quick five minutes. The explosion led the news at seven and ten and was the second piece at eleven. Each bulletin added little snippets of new information that helped her to colour in between the lines.

The Impala was rumoured to have been stolen in New Jersey thirteen months earlier.

It had been seen at a drive-thru restaurant just outside of Philadelphia.

Local businesses had reported suspicious sales of fertiliser.

And, then, at one in the morning, more detail. The bulletin included a still of the suspect that had been taken by a security camera at the drive-thru.

Isabella stared at grainy footage of herself, standing before the counter, collecting a bag of food and three drinks.

She switched off the television, undressed and slipped between the crisp sheets.

It was settled then.

It would have to be tomorrow.

She couldn't stay any longer than that.

They would be looking now, and it wouldn't be long until they found her.

Chapter Twenty-One

Isabella awoke at six the following morning. She had plenty to do, and it paid to start early.

She went into the bathroom and stood under the shower for ten minutes, clearing away the last remnants of sleep. She closed her eyes and tried to place everything into context. She stepped out of the shower and dried herself off. She took a pair of nail scissors from her mother's bag and used them to cut her hair. The scissors were not suited to the task, but she worked as carefully as she could, following a line that sheared off most of her blonde locks and left her with a page-boy cut that ended just above the nape of her neck. She swept the hair up and deposited it into the waste bin.

She took out the packet of hair dye and the jar of Vaseline. She wrapped a towel around her shoulders and put on the thin latex gloves that came in the packet. She coated her hairline, ears and neck with the Vaseline. She combed her hair into four different sections, fixed them with clips, and then applied the dye to her hair, working it in with her fingers. She had never done anything like this before, but she had read the instructions carefully and watched several YouTube fashion how-to videos on her cellphone and was confident that she knew what she was doing. She left the dye to penetrate, and then, when it had, she held her head under the shower head, running hot water through her hair. When she was done, and the water was running clear, she dried herself and looked in the mirror.

Her hair was the same cut and colour as Cassidy's.

Good.

She packed her mother's things back into the bag. She worked quickly and thoroughly, ensuring that nothing was left behind. She zipped the bag up and took it, together with the bag of hair clippings and the packaging for the hair dye, outside to the fenced-off area where the hotel's bins were kept. She pushed back the lid on the nearest unit and, standing on tiptoes, tossed both bags inside. She closed the lid again and went back to the room.

She took her own case and collected her things. She didn't have very much, and it didn't take long.

She wheeled the case to the door and stopped to look back one final time. She was satisfied that the room was clean enough. There would be fingerprints, true, and there was nothing that could easily be done about that, but she had never been fingerprinted before, and so she was not concerned about detection. The staff and other guests would be able to identify her picture, but that, too, did not worry her. She didn't plan on sticking around for very long.

She took Cassidy's jacket and put it on, and then stepped outside.

There was just one final thing that she needed to do.

Isabella took a taxi back to the mall. She paid the driver with a twenty, tipping him the change.

"Will you wait for me?" she asked him.

"Sure, but I'll need to keep the meter running."

"That's alright. I won't be long."

She walked across the sidewalk into the air-conditioned climate inside the store.

She had memorised the things she needed. She took a trolley and set off, heading for the large Target.

Inside, her first stop was the clothing section. She walked the aisles quickly, depositing a beige cable-knit jumper, a plaid skirt, a pair of thick knitted tights, a pair of trainers and a knitted beanie like the one that Cassidy had been wearing. She added a second outfit: checked shirt, black Levis, a pair of Converse All Stars, and a mesh cap. She added a pair of clear glasses with a thick black plastic frame and a colourful canvas satchel.

Satisfied with her purchases, she paid at the counter and stopped in the customer restroom to change. She put on the tights, skirt and sweater. She put on Cassidy's leather jacket again. She folded her old clothes neatly and pressed them into the trash.

She went into one of the stalls and shut the door. She opened the case and took out the Beretta Nano. She examined the gun carefully, pulled out the six-shot magazine and checked that it was fully loaded. It was, with another round in the pipe. Seven shots, total.

She pushed the magazine back into the gun.

She stopped at the mirror and put on the beanie, arranging it so that her newly trimmed and dyed hair was obscured beneath it. She would never pass for Cassidy—she was too young and the older girl was too pretty—but there were similarities now. Hair, eyes, clothing. It might be enough. Maybe. She reached into the jacket pocket and took out a ten-dollar bill, a packet of tissues, a New York City driver's license and a library card. She put the note in her pocket, discarded the tissues and put the two cards back again.

It might.

She took the bag with the second outfit and went back outside to the cab.

"I'm waiting for someone," the driver said when she opened the door.

"Yes," she said. "Me."

He looked at her and smiled. "That was a fast change. Didn't recognise you."

She smiled sweetly at him.

"Where to?"

"Do you know Sentara Norfolk General Hospital?"

"Sure I do, sugar. Up in Ghent."

"There, please."

———

The hospital was eight miles north of Chesapeake. Isabella had the taxi stop a block away from it and walked the rest of the way there. It was nine in the morning and already looking like it was going to be a fine day, bright and with the first stirrings of spring. Isabella didn't pay it much attention. She was focussed and deliberate, quite clear about what she had to do.

The hospital was a big, modern building, affiliated with the Eastern Virginia Medical School that was alongside it. Ambulances were queued up at the side of the road, and taxis buzzed in and out of the traffic. A steady stream of pedestrians headed through the big open doors that led into the lobby.

She walked up to the wide plate glass doors and waited for them to part. She continued inside, quickly acclimating herself: a broad reception desk, ranks of comfortable chairs for those who were waiting, wide windows that looked out onto a pretty orna-mental garden. Several corridors led away from the central area and she saw signs for the cafeteria and for departments that offered treatments for various ailments.

A woman in a nurse's uniform stopped and smiled at her.

"Are you lost, honey?"

"A bit," she said, shyly. "I'm looking for the burns unit."

The woman pointed to the elevators. "You want to take the elevator to the third floor and follow the signs. You won't be able to miss it."

"Thank you."

"Who are you here to see?"

"My father," she said.

"What's your name?"

"Cassidy."

The woman was just being pleasant. Her deceit was wasted on her. "Alright, Cassidy. I hope he's alright."

Chapter Twenty-Two

Michael Pope pulled into the parking lot next to the hospital and killed the hire car's engine. It was still early, and the lot was reasonably quiet, mostly staff arriving for the daytime shift.

He sat quietly for a moment, assessing his surroundings with an experienced and cautious eye. There was an outside broadcast truck from WCTV parked up in the row nearest to the exit. That was the only sign that the hospital counted the victim of the explosion among its patients. There had been reporters from the major networks on-site in the immediate aftermath of the blast, but they had all been recalled now that the story had started to go cold. That was the reality of the news cycle: there was always something more interesting just down the track.

Pope picked up his cellphone and dialled.

It connected and rang for ten seconds before it was picked up.

"Global Logistics," the female operator responded.

"I'd like to speak to the managing director, please."

"May I ask who's calling?"

"It's Michael Pope."

"Please hold, sir."

Pope had arrived in Virginia that night. He had flown to Philadelphia, hired the car and then driven south, stopping only to meet the Group Fifteen quartermaster so that he could be equipped. He had listened to news radio as he drove south. The explosion was mentioned a few times, but it had quickly been subsumed by other stories. He had supplemented his understanding in a call with the two MI5 spooks who had arrived in theatre two days before him. They were already in Chesapeake and had made extensive enquiries with local reporters. They were able to confirm what Pope had already suspected: Beatrix Rose was dead, and she had very nearly taken Control with her.

Nearly, but not quite.

The call connected.

"Hello." The greeting was clipped and brusque. It sounded like speaking to Pope was the last thing that Sir Benjamin Stone, the head of the Secret Intelligence Service, wanted to be doing.

"I'm here."

"You took your time."

"There's a lot happening."

"Well?"

"He's not dead. She triggered a bomb, but he's not dead. Can't have been close enough to it."

"Injured, though?"

"Burns."

"Prognosis?"

"Not life threatening. He'll make it."

"But you'll see that he doesn't?"

"Yes, sir."

"What about our friend?"

"She's dead."

"Have they identified her?"

"No. And it won't be easy. They've got a picture of her, but I doubt they'll be able to match it up with anything. She's been careful, and she's been off the grid for ten years. She was a ghost."

"So we're in the clear?"

"Not necessarily. They've got a picture of her daughter. They've circulated it."

There was mild disbelief in his voice. "She took her out there with her?"

"It looks like it, sir."

He heard the man's temper flickering. "Why couldn't she make it easy for us, just for once? Where is she now?"

"The locals don't know. But this is a thirteen-year-old girl, sir, on her own in a country she doesn't know. She can't hide forever. We have to assume they'll pick her up eventually. And then it'll just be a question of what she knows."

Pope heard his consternation. "What a bloody mess."

He glanced in the wing mirror and saw the man in a white coat approaching the car. He walked around to the passenger side door, opened it and slid inside.

"I have to go now, sir," Pope said.

"Keep me posted."

Stone ended the call.

Pope put the cellphone away and turned to the man on the seat next to him.

"Hello, Pope," John Milton said.

"Hello, Milton. Thanks for coming. You didn't have to."

Milton shook his head, dismissing it. "No, I did," he said. "I owe her, too, remember. We'd both be dead if she hadn't turned up when she did. And I have a debt to settle with him, too. The world will be a better place without him in it."

"Yes," Pope said. "My thoughts entirely."

171

Milton had sworn off his old line of work, and although Pope would have dearly loved to have a man like him in the Group again, he had known, with certainty, that his entreaties would have been wasted on him. He wasn't interested in pushing his luck, either. He respected Milton's reasons. He was the best assassin that Pope had ever seen, until he had met Beatrix, and he had a lot of blood on his hands. More than the others in the Group. He was trying to make amends for it.

Milton was wearing a doctor's coat with ID pinned to the lapel.

"Where did you get that?" Pope asked.

"I've been inside. I found a locker."

"Did you look around?"

He nodded. "He's up there. Third floor."

"How is he?"

"They say seventy per cent burns. He's not in a good way, but they got him in quickly enough. He won't look like much when they're done with him, but he'll recover."

"Have you seen him?"

He shook his head. "There's security outside the room. It's not going to be easy."

"How many men?"

"Two," he said. "Manage Risk employees, both armed. Police, too."

He was right. It wouldn't be easy.

"This is your gig," Milton said. "What do you want to do?"

"One of us causes a diversion, the other one takes him out."

"You have a preference?"

"You have more history with him than I do."

Pope looked into Milton's eyes—bluish grey, determined, pitiless. Milton didn't have many friends, and Pope was probably the best of them. But even their friendship, the time they had spent together throughout the years, had not insulated him from the shiver that he always felt when he was fixed in that ironclad stare.

Milton nodded. There was no need for anything else.

"Come on, then," Pope said. "Let's get started."

He opened the door and went around to the trunk. He opened it and unzipped the small bag that was inside. There were two Sig P226 S4s inside the bag, both fitted with Trident 9 suppressors. Pope had checked them both out in the deserted parking lot where he had met the quartermaster. The actions felt crisp. Nice and solid. The suppressors were both reasonably new. They might not even have been fired before.

He reached into the bag and took out a third item: a lead-lined case that contained a syringe and a transparent ampoule holding two milligrams of polonium-210 dissolved in 3.3ml of saline. Polonium was an effective and convenient poison. It emitted pure alpha particles, which, outside of the body, could be stopped by a sheet of tissue paper. Inside the body, however, it was something else. The radiation released energy that created free radicals, and they, in turn, formed toxic compounds that degraded surrounding cells.

Death was guaranteed, quick and difficult to diagnose. In a case like this, it would most likely be attributed to existing trauma.

It was the perfect poison.

The KGB had loved it.

"Think you can get into the room?"

Milton took the case and slipped it into his pocket. "Yes," he said.

Chapter Twenty-Three

Something had stirred Control. They had him dosed up to the eyeballs with liquid morphine, and the opiate had filled his brain with a thick, somnolent haze. It took five minutes for him to realise that he was awake.

It took another moment to realise where he was.

And then another to remember what had happened to him.

Cassidy's telephone call had saved his life. It had given him the chance to put a little distance between himself and the seat of the explosion, and because of that, he had been spared the obliteration that Beatrix Rose had intended for them both. Instead, the shockwave from the detonation had picked him up and flung him against the side of the Little Bird. The impact had broken his arm and three of his ribs. The firestorm had swept over him next, a rolling tide of flame that had incinerated his clothes and his hair and cooked his skin.

He could remember only occasional moments in the hours that had followed. An ambulance had taken him to the nearest emergency room, but when they assessed the scale of the damage, it was clear that he needed more specialised treatment. He had come around from his drugged stupor long enough to remember being dunked in a stainless steel tub of iced water. They had given him morphine again, but he had been awake long enough to recall the burned skin being cut away from his face and chest and the front of his legs. They had slathered him with burn cream, wrapped him in bandages and then transferred him to Sentara.

The bandages had been removed, and his body had been soaked in ice water before an anti-bacterial solution was applied. He was moved to an isolation ward while his wounds were left to air-dry, and then more cream was applied and the wounds bandaged again. The procedure would be repeated, day and night, for as long as it took. Weeks, maybe.

The morphine was a constant. His senses were blunted and dulled, and in those hours when he was awake, it often felt as if he was underwater.

He had unconsciously scratched at his wounds during the night, and so the nurses had fastened ties around his wrists to stop him. They were attached now, his arms secured down by his sides. He struggled instinctively before remembering what had happened and then relaxed.

"Daddy?"

He opened his eyes. Cassidy was sitting in the chair next to his bed.

"Can you hear me, Daddy?"

He tried to speak, but his lips and mouth were dry. Cassidy stood and took a sponge from a bowl of water on the table next to the chair. She held the sponge over his mouth and squeezed gently. Drops of moisture rolled into his mouth.

"Thank you," he rasped.

"How are you feeling?"

"Sleepy . . ."

The drugs. They said that was to be expected."

He closed his eyes, and sleep welled up around him again.

"Daddy?"

"I'm . . . I'm . . ."

"Try and stay awake for a little bit."

He opened his eyes again. Cassidy was standing there, smiling down at him.

"The doctors are pleased with how it's going. They say they'll need to operate again next week. They'll have to cut away until they can get to the new skin beneath. And then they say they'll look at grafts."

"What . . . what do I look like?"

The flicker of uncertainty that passed across her lovely face was enough. "You look like you've been in an explosion. But the doctors are pleased with how you're healing. They seem optimistic."

He knew that was all for his benefit, but he tried to smile his understanding, forgetting that his mouth was hidden beneath the bandages and that, in any event, the effort of using those muscles and flexing his charred skin was too painful.

He gasped and she leaned in closer, concern on her face. "Are you alright?"

"Yes."

"Can I get you anything?"

"No."

"Alright, then. I'm going to go and tell them that you're awake. Your bandages need to be changed."

He tried to reach out a hand for her, but the stays held his arm in place. "Cassidy," he whispered.

"What is it?"

"Your mother?"

"She's coming. The boys, too. Their flight gets in tonight. I'm going to meet them at the airport. I'll bring them straight over."

"Thank you."

She waited at the foot of the bed.

"Beatrix Rose?"

"You asked last night, Daddy. She's dead. Burnt to a crisp."

"Good."

"You don't need to worry about her any more. She can rot in Hell."

"And the girl . . . ?"

"They don't know where she is. They're still looking. They'll find her. She's just a girl. How hard can it be?"

The elevator reached the third floor. There was a soft chime, the doors opened and Isabella stepped out into the lobby. It was an open space bounded at both ends by glass walls with automatic doors. She tightened her grip on the handle of the canvas bag and went through the door to the right.

A teenage girl and a man were walking along the corridor towards her. Isabella recognised the girl at once.

Cassidy.

She didn't know the man. He was of medium height. His hair was cut short, very close to the scalp on the sides and just a little longer on top. He was wearing a suit that looked expensive. His shoes looked expensive, too. They were polished so deeply that the strip lights overhead glittered off the caps.

They were talking, and they didn't see her.

There was an open door immediately to her left. Isabella slipped inside. It was a small waiting area, with a table and chairs, magazines fanned out on the table. The kind of place where the family of patients who were critically ill might be asked to wait. She stayed near the door.

She held her breath and waited.

She dared a glance outside.

There was a larger waiting area where several long leather couches had been arranged, facing a picture window that offered a panoramic view of the Chesapeake skyline. The man and the girl had taken seats there. They were pointed away from her, facing the window.

She frowned with frustration. She took off the beanie and the leather jacket and stuffed them into the bin. So much for her brilliant plan.

They continued their conversation. Isabella was close enough to eavesdrop on them.

"So how was he?" she heard the man ask.

"Awake."

"But?"

"But he's in a bad way. He's covered head to toe in bandages, and they've had to tie his arms down to stop him clawing."

"I've seen soldiers with burns before. You'd be surprised. It's amazing what they can do these days."

"The doctors are fantastic. I'm very grateful for what you're doing. The money . . . it must be . . ."

"Don't be crazy. It's the least we can do."

"Has he spoken about what happened?"

"No, not really. They pump him full of morphine practically all the time. He asks about her, though."

"She won't be a problem anymore. She's gone. That's one thing we can be sure about. You need to tell him that."

"I do."

Isabella tightened her grip on the handle of the bag. A nurse walked down the corridor towards her. She took a seat, dropped the bag and fumbled a magazine from the table.

The nurse stopped at the door.

"Is everything alright, honey?"

"Yes," she said.

"Is there anything I can do to help?"

"No," she said, wishing the woman would stop drawing attention to her.

"Who are you here to see?"

"My father," she said.

"What? Mr Finnegan?"

Isabella flinched, terrified that Cassidy or the other man would hear, be suspicious, find her out. Her mouth was suddenly dry and she could only manage a shallow nod.

The nurse looked puzzled. Isabella's stomach contracted with nerves.

"Mr Finnegan? Your big sister is here. I just saw her."

"Yes," she said, managing a smile, but struggling to tamp down her fright. "I know."

"Why are you in here, then? Are you alright?"

Leave me alone. "I'm fine, really," she said.

She woman's pager buzzed. She picked it up, looked at it and nodded to herself.

"I've got to run," she said, smiling back at her. "But if you or your sister need anything, I'm just at the desk at the end of the corridor. My name's Megan. You just need to ask."

"Thank you," Isabella said.

The woman walked to the desk.

Too close.

She needed to do better. Couldn't leave it to dumb luck like that. She wouldn't last long if that was the best that she could do.

She strained her ears again.

"He asked about the girl," Cassidy was saying.

"We have something on that. She was in a hotel fifteen minutes from here. The staff recognised her picture. She checked out this morning."

She sounded panicked. "What does that mean . . . ?"

"It doesn't mean anything," the man said in a calming tone. "I don't want you to worry, Cassidy. The chances are she's just trying to work out how to get home, and when she goes to the airport, and she will go there, the police will pick her up. In the meantime, I'm going to tell the guards to look out for her and increase the security detail from two to four. Around the clock, twenty-four-seven." He lowered his voice a little. "You need to remember that she's just a girl. The mother was dangerous. The daughter? I'm pretty sure we can handle the daughter."

Isabella watched their reflections in the window as first the man and then Cassidy stood.

"Would he recognise me if I went in?" the man asked.

"I don't think so. The drugs . . ."

"Of course. I won't, then. But tell him I stopped by. And you need to remember that we will do everything we can to put him back together. *Everything*, alright? Money is no object here."

"Thank you, Mr King. I can't begin to tell you how grateful I am. My whole family is grateful."

The man leaned down to her and kissed her on the cheek. "It's not a problem. Now, come on. Come downstairs with me. You need a break. Let me buy you some coffee."

Isabella hid behind the door, listening to the sound of their footsteps as they walked back to the elevators.

She waited a moment, checked that the space outside was empty and then emerged and walked quickly in the opposite direction.

⌣

They went in through the main door. Pope went first and took stock. He recognised the reporter from WCTV, drinking coffee with her crew in the cafeteria. There were two uniformed cops on the table next to them, one of them leaning over and flirting with her as she tried to tease out nuggets of new information. A man at an adjacent table was working on a laptop; a print reporter, perhaps? A policeman, fat and out of shape, was sitting on a stool, drinking coffee from an outsized Styrofoam cup. A young, slender, pretty girl was waiting as a man brought two coffees over from the counter. Pope recognised him as Jamie King from Manage Risk.

There were two men who looked like they might have been soldiers once upon a time. Easy to spot. They were Manage Risk operatives keeping an eye on the comings and goings down here. Add to that the two men that Milton had seen upstairs.

Four men, at least.

Not going to be easy.

But nothing worthwhile ever was.

He paused and looked back. Milton had followed him inside. He moved confidently, as if he knew exactly what he was doing and where he was going, as if he had important business to attend to, as if he belonged here. He looked like a doctor, although Pope knew that the pretence would fold under even the most nominal scrutiny. They would have to hope that didn't happen.

Milton walked straight to the elevators.

Pope followed and, checking that he was unobserved, opened the door to the stairs. A flight of concrete steps went up; another flight went down.

There was an emergency panel fitted to the wall next to the door.

Pope covered his fist with his shirt sleeve and listened for the sound of Milton's elevator ascending the shaft.

Here we go.

He counted to ten, smashed the glass and, his finger still covered by the shirt, activated the alarm.

All Control wanted to do was sleep, but there was a noise, a ringing, that faded in and out of the narcotic fugue. He closed his eyes and let his head settle back into the soft pillows. The pain flashed again, and he pressed the trigger near to his hand to administer another dose. The morphine dripped into the line in his arm, a narcotic feed that wrapped him in its warm, fuzzy embrace and encouraged his dreams and memories.

The ringing faded away.

The pain, too.

He closed his eyes and found himself transported back to years earlier. He was in his old office, with the wide view of the Thames. The water was green and the sky gunmetal grey. The red buses that ferried to and fro on the other side of the water looked hyper-real, a glowing crimson rather than the usual dowdy red.

Control had Beatrix Rose's file spread out on the desk in front of him. A vacancy had arisen, and she had been proposed. She had been a rising star in the military back then, destined for high rank, but he had other plans for her.

He picked up one of the photographs that had been taken during the week-long surveillance that was a crucial element of the vetting process. There was a coldness in her face, a clinical aspect that he would come to admire, but beyond all that, she was beautiful. Very beautiful. Long, straight blonde hair, alabaster skin, extraordinarily blue eyes.

The haze shifted, became grey and dense, and when it cleared, he was still in the chair behind the desk, but now she was sitting opposite him.

"Hello, Miss Rose."

"Hello, sir."

"Thank you for coming to see me. Do you know why you're here?"

"Only vaguely, I'm afraid."

"I am responsible for a classified government agency. I say 'government', but it's not something that could ever be acknowledged outside these walls. If what we do in the name of the state ever came to light, it would be . . . well, it would be particularly uncomfortable."

"Like I said, sir, I'm a little in the dark."

"What have you been told, Miss Rose?"

"Just that there's a chance I might be offered a transfer. A new position. That's all, really."

"Yes," he had said. "That's right. A transfer."

"A transfer to what?"

"Let me ask you a hypothetical question. If you were given an order to kill someone, would you do it?"

"What has this person done?"

"That's irrelevant."

"They might not think so."

"You don't know anything about them."

"Are we at war?"

"No."

"Who gave me the order?"

"Let's say I did."

"Your orders would be that I had to murder someone?"

"That's an emotive word."

"But that's what it would be. Killing in peacetime. Murder."

"I'd prefer to call it employment."

A thin smile.

"Would you do it without question, without hesitation, without doubt?"

She looked at him, sizing him up.

"Would you do it, Miss Rose?"

He remembered how she had paused, fixing him in that lizard gaze, the eyes that held no emotion, and he knew then with utter conviction, that she was perfect for the purpose to which he would put her.

"Yes, sir," she said. "I would."

The clouds washed up again like surf breaking across a beach, drowning his memory.

When it faded, and he opened his eyes, Beatrix Rose was sitting in the chair next to the bed. She had one of her wicked throwing knives in her right hand, the index finger of her left hand stroking its razored edge, a thin cut on her fingertip already filling with blood. She was looking at him, her glacial blue eyes passionless and pitiless, and as he stared back, his insides turning molten, sweat soaking his bandages, he thought he saw the beginning of a smile curling up at the edges of her ashen lips.

He fumbled for the button to call the nurse, to call security, to call *anyone*. His fingers crabbed across the linen, questing for it, but his wrists were restrained and the range of his finger was curtailed, and as he looked back up again in terror, he saw that the chair was empty again, and he realised he was still suspended in the kaleidoscope of opiate dreams.

He breathed in and out, his heartbeat slowly returning to a normal rate.

Beatrix.

She had been an incredible agent. His most valuable asset then.

Only John Milton could have competed with her.

And he had erred with both of them.

The consequences of his error had been sadistic and remorseless.

Beatrix and five other agents with whom she had served were dead.

Was it his fault?

Milton had succumbed to doubts and demons. Control might have spotted that earlier, done something to prevent the escalation, but he couldn't blame himself for another man's weaknesses.

But Beatrix Rose?

Yes.

That *had* been his fault. That had been the fault of his greed.

It had been such a terrible shame that it had all gone so badly wrong.

He twitched involuntarily, and scraping his arm across the sheet, he reached for the morphine trigger again.

Chapter Twenty-Four

Cassidy and the other man had emerged from a door at the end of the floor. Isabella approached it and looked through the glass panel. A corridor reached back with four doors set into it. Two men stood at the end of the corridor.

Big men.

Big men with guns.

She slowed her step.

The men shifted, shuffled their feet. They were in front of one of the doors. There was no way to get past them.

She floundered.

Her plan had been to pretend to be the man's daughter.

She realised now that wouldn't work. She recalled the conversation she had overhead. They knew she was out there. They would be wary.

She suddenly realised that she did not know what she should do.

The fire alarm suddenly sounded, loud and shrill.

Isabella stopped, waiting for the alarm to stop.

A drill?

A mistake?

But it didn't stop. It kept ringing.

One man turned to the other and said something. The other man turned, looked down the corridor to the door, saw her looking in through the glass panel, took a quarter turn in her direction, held her eye.

Isabella thought of her mother.

Her poor mother, torn away from her, sent into solitude for years because of the man in the room just a few feet away from her.

She was too far along the path to let fear distract her now.

They might be wary, but there was no way that they could anticipate *this*.

Isabella reached into the bag and wrapped her fingers around the little Beretta. She pushed the door open and approached the guards. They were dressed in dark suits and white shirts with smart, well-polished shoes. They were tall and looked powerful. They looked like soldiers. Both had bulges beneath their left armpits. Isabella knew what those were.

The men turned to look at her. They had been told to be cautious, but, even so, she was just a young girl, a sweet and pretty young girl, and that brought a host of expectations. The idea that she might be a threat to them took a moment to process, and that moment was all that she needed.

"You can't come in here," one of them said, raising a hand. He turned to face her, blocking the way ahead, presenting a nice, wide target.

She stepped closer, pulled the gun clear of the bag and, with him just a handful of feet away, fired twice. The first round went through his upraised hand into his chest and the second hit him in the throat. He toppled backwards onto his backside, his eyes bulging with astonishment, pressing at the pulsating fold of skin in his throat, blood already running out of it, running through the hole in his hand.

The second man took a half step back, his hand fumbling inside his jacket and fiddling with the retention strap that held his weapon in its holster. It should have been a simple, practiced routine, the thumb flicking the strap before the fingers pulled the gun, but he couldn't do it. The incongruity of what he had just seen had stunned the knowledge out of him.

Isabella took two steps to confront him.

And fired again.

He tumbled backwards into the room.

Isabella followed.

———

Control heard the noises from outside: a quick pop, something heavy dropping to the floor, scuffling feet, a second pop.

He opened his eyes just as a man's body bumped open the door and fell backwards into the room.

A young girl followed the man across the threshold.

She was pointing a semi-automatic pistol at him.

She pointed down at him and fired once, cleanly and efficiently, and the man jerked once and then lay still.

The girl returned to the door and dragged the body of a second man into the room. He was much bigger than she, and she struggled. She hauled him inside far enough that she could close the door.

Control tried to move, thrashing his arms in sudden panic, but the ties around his wrists jerked tight, and all he succeeded in doing was pressing himself back into the bed.

The girl walked across the room.

She took a pillow and held it over his chest.

She pressed the muzzle of the gun against the pillow.

"This is for my father."

She pulled the trigger.

Pfft.

It felt as if someone had punched him in the gut.

The morphine meant that he didn't feel the pain. It felt as if he had been winded.

"And this is for my mother."

She pulled the trigger again.

Pfft.

Another punch in the chest.

He gasped for breath that didn't come. He watched as the girl looked over him, then followed her eyes as she glanced to the bank of medical equipment to the side of the bed. His blood pressure was falling even as his pulse spiked. A feeling of awful emptiness grew in his chest, and his breath came faster and faster. A curtain of darkness seemed near, just at the edge of his vision, and when he blinked and opened his eyes again, it seemed nearer still. He opened and closed his mouth, trying to speak. The words were irrelevant, just sibilant noises, and then it was as if he had been tipped over into that pit of blackness.

The last thing he registered was the girl, still standing over him.

Her eyes were wintry, icy blue, impassionate and unsparing.

His last thought, as the light leeched away from the edges of his vision, and the cowl of darkness started to descend, was that her cold blue eyes were just like her mother's.

Isabella moved quickly.

She took off the jumper and skirt and changed into the check shirt and Levis. She took out the red mesh cap and put it on her head, then dumped the first outfit in the bin by the sink.

She wiped the Beretta down, removing her prints, and dropped it into the bin, too.

She checked her reflection in the mirror above the sink. She straightened her darkened hair and dabbed a piece of moist tissue against the drop of blood that had found its way onto her cheek. She cleaned it away. Nothing was out of place.

She took a breath and opened the door. The corridor was empty. The alarm was still sounding. There was a patch of bloody blowback on the door. She returned to the room, collected a tissue and scrubbed it away. Then, satisfied, she walked briskly to the elevator lobby.

The nearest elevator pinged, and the doors opened. Two men, much like the two she had shot, emerged from the car and walked briskly towards the door from which she had just exited. They looked troubled.

A door to the right of the elevator doors was marked with a sign that said it led to the emergency stairs. Isabella pushed through it.

The flight of stairs headed down, but she found she couldn't move. She felt dizzy, lightheaded and weak, and she had to put out a hand against the wall to steady herself.

She heard the sound of angry voices from the other side of the door, and then the noise of running feet.

She pushed herself away from the wall and started down the stairs. They suddenly looked too much for her to negotiate. She took a step, unsteadily, clinging onto the rail, and then another. She was almost at the half-landing when she felt the bile surge up from her stomach, burning up her gullet and filling her mouth. She vomited, dropping to the floor as the hot sick poured out of her mouth and pooled around her knees. She swiped the back of her hand across her mouth, trying to scrub it all away, but now her jeans were covered with it, and she still felt weak.

She had killed three men.

Killed them.

Murdered them?

Her mother hadn't told her how it would feel.

She hadn't told her it would feel like this.

She tried to stand, but the weakness washed over her again.
She couldn't.
Couldn't move.
Couldn't.

Chapter Twenty-Five

The elevator doors opened, and the sound of the alarm, which had been muffled, flooded inside, loud and strident. Milton marched purposefully into the third floor lobby. He knew how to behave. How to look. *You belong here. This is all second nature.*

He had skirted the floor earlier, observing judiciously, setting everything in his mind's eye so that when he returned he would waste no time orientating himself; the lobby, with the glass walls with automatic doors; the waiting area with the long leather couches; the picture window with the view of the Chesapeake skyline.

Milton went through the glass doors.

The space beyond was empty.

He walked quickly to the door that led to the corridor where Control was being treated.

The door opened.

A big man bustled out of it.

A second man was behind him.

Both of them were carrying pistols.

Milton started to change course.

"Hey," the first man called out to him.

Milton stopped. "Yes?"

"Who are you?"

"Doctor Cromartie. Who are you?"

The second man slipped around them both and ran for the lobby.

"Have you seen anyone up here?"

"No," Milton said. He gestured down at the pistol. "What's going on?"

The second man disappeared into the lobby.

"Have you seen anyone?" the man asked again.

"I told you, no. I've only just come up."

Milton assessed: he had a minute, two if he was lucky.

No time to play it any other way.

He punched the man in the gut, as hard as he could. His eyes went wide as saucers as he bent double, folding over the blow. As his chin descended, Milton brought up his leg. His knee connected with the man's chin, the impact sudden and unsparing. The man blacked out, unconscious, even before he had crumpled to the floor.

Milton stepped over him. He drew the Sig P226 that Pope had given him and, his finger on the trigger, pushed the door open and hurried into the corridor.

He cleared the rooms one by one.

Empty.

Empty.

Empty.

He reached the last door, pushing it open with the toe of his boot.

An identical room, same as the others. Bed, chair, medical equipment.

But two men were on the floor. Both of them had been shot. Blood still oozed from the wounds.

He looked up at the bed.

A man, swaddled in bandages, his wrists fastened to fabric ties. There he was.

Control.

He stepped up to the bed.

Two entry wounds in his chest. The edges were cauterised. Powder burns. The gun had been fired at close range.

Milton had seen enough. He went back into the corridor, stepped over the unconscious man and made his way back onto the main area of the third floor. He flipped the tails of his doctor's coat aside, shoved the P226 into the back of his trousers and let the coat fall over it.

Four men burst through the glass doors. They were all armed, weapons out.

"Help!" Milton yelled. "Help! In there!"

The men pushed by on either side and ran down the corridor.

Milton hurried to the elevators. The doors to the nearest one were closing. He reached into the narrowing gap, pushed them back and stepped inside.

———

Pope's phone was on silent, and it buzzed urgently in his pocket.

He took it out and pressed it to his ear.

"What is it?"

"He's already dead."

"What do you mean?"

Milton's voice was clipped, disciplined. "I looked inside. Both guards were shot. I checked him and he's been shot, too. Two rounds, in the chest, close range. Professional."

"Shot by who?"

"I've no idea."

"Where are you?"

"Outside. They've got four men up there already, and there'll be more on the way. Where are you?"

"Ground floor."

"Get out now."

"I will."

"You still need me?"

"No. It's done."

"Copy that."

"Good luck, Milton."

"And you."

Pope ended the call and put the cellphone back in his pocket.

He looked at his watch. He had been here for ten minutes. Already more than he would have preferred. The stairwell had been busy for the first few minutes as staff and visitors evacuated.

He was turning to go when he heard the sound of retching on the landing above him.

He reached inside his jacket for the Sig and pushed his shoulders against the wall. He started up the stairs, one at a time, the gun raised next to his cheek and his finger curled around the trigger, ready to fire.

He had taken ten steps upwards when he saw the girl on the floor.

She was crawling in his direction, on hands and knees, vomit plastered across her face.

He stopped, his muscles throbbing with coiled energy, adrenaline flooding his blood, his every instinct, hardwired from years of combat, telling him that he needed to get out of the hospital and he needed to do it now, right this second, and yet he didn't. He stayed.

Because as she looked up at him he recognised her.

"*Isabella?*"

She froze.

His brain flashed and joined the dots.

She had killed Control?

She was Beatrix's fallback?

Holy shit.

Beatrix had left behind one hell of a legacy.

The girl scrabbled backwards, panic on her face.

"Hey," he said, quickly shoving the Sig away and holding up his empty hands. "Hey, relax, it's alright. I knew your mother. I came to see her once, in Marrakech. You've met me before. We had dinner together. Remember?"

The girl scrambled all the way back across the half-landing, her back bumping up against the wall.

"I know what's happened. I know what you've done. We need to get you out, right now."

She hugged her arms around her chest.

There was suddenly a clatter as the door above was thrown violently open, crashing back against the wall, and two men rushed onto the landing.

Soldiers.

Pope's hand was moving to his holster even as they turned and looked down at them on the half-landing.

"Hey!" one of them called down to them as Pope's fingers snagged the grip, pulled the gun out in a smooth sideways motion, aimed and fired. The suppressor barked, the bullet travelling the short distance between them in a flash, terminating its flight in the man's stomach. He gasped, clutched his midriff and dropped to his knees, exposing the second man, and Pope nudged his aim to the left and fired again. The bullet tore into his leg, punching it out from underneath him. He toppled over the stairs and rolled down them, an abrupt crack marking the moment when he snapped the vertebrae in his neck. The first man, gut shot, tried to raise his semi-automatic, but Pope fired a third and final time. His head splashed red and grey, and he jack-knifed over onto his back, pivoting at the hips, arms wide.

The second man's body slithered down the steps, coming to a rest next to Isabella. His arm was trapped beneath his body, his legs pointed straight back up the stairs, and his head was twisted at a perverse angle.

Isabella screamed and clasped her hands over her face.

Pope holstered the gun again, hurried across to her and knelt down.

"It's alright," he reassured her. "It's alright."

She didn't respond and her hands stayed where they were.

"I can get you out of here, Isabella. You want to get out?

She nodded, still silent.

"But if we don't go now, they'll find you. There'll be more men like them. I'm sure your mother told you what you needed to do, and how to get away, but you're running out of time. We've got minutes, that's all. We have to go. Now."

The girl took her hands away and looked up at him fearfully. How old was she? Thirteen? Fourteen? She looked much younger.

"Come on. Your mother wouldn't want this."

He reached out and laid a hand on her shoulder.

He thought she might shrug it away, but she didn't.

"You can trust me, Isabella."

Pope opened the door to the elevator lobby. He scanned quickly: the alarm was still ringing, much louder down here, and staff and visitors were dutifully filing towards the exits. They moved quickly and purposefully, calmly, no panic. They probably thought it was a drill.

That was good.

He took his suppressed Sig and dropped it into the trash.

"Do you have your gun?"

She shook her head.

"Where is it?"

"In the room. The bin."

"Good."

He reached down and scooped Isabella into his arms. He had cleaned the vomit away as best as he could, but she was pale faced and looked as if she could faint at any time. He walked out into the atrium, past the reception desk, and merged at the back of the queue of people. The girl was small in his arms, her skin cool and slender, and she was holding on tight.

Pope was going to get her out.

He owed Beatrix that, at least.

She had saved his life once, far away.

This would square the ledger.

The two of them drew closer to the revolving doors.

He watched as two police cruisers raced up the access road and screeched to a sudden stop.

They entered the revolving door, the girl pressed up close to him as he shuffled around.

The doors opened and four officers exited.

Come on.

The door revolved, and they were outside, the cool air on their faces.

Calm. Stay calm.

Pope concentrated on looking as normal as he could. The fact that they were together made it less likely that they would be stopped. What were they, after all? A father and his daughter, leaving the hospital just like all the others around them. She was weak or upset. Nothing unusual. No reason to give them a second glance.

An SUV with blacked-out windows and the crossed gladii logo of Manage Risk raced up the access road and stopped next to the police cruisers. Three operatives got out and hurried into the hospital.

Another SUV was racing to the hospital along the main road.

They would be swamped soon. Drowning in ex-special forces operatives who had probably already been told that the explosion and what had happened to Control was an act of terrorism.

Operatives who would, very likely, have a predisposition towards shooting first and clearing up the mess later.

Pope walked briskly to the parking lot and, with one hand, opened the passenger door to the rental. He lowered Isabella into the seat and buckled her up. He checked the mirrors, saw that the lot was clear and started the engine. The second SUV swept into the lot, and Pope drove slowly around it, gently accelerating away.

Chapter Twenty-Six

The place she was looking for was not far from the Jemma el Fna. Isabella had the address on a piece of paper. It was in her mother's neat and tidy handwriting, and she looked at it often. Not because she had forgotten where she was going, but because it reminded her of her mother. She had found the piece of paper in her mother's bag.

She reached a grocery store with a brothel above it. She stopped and checked the address again. Two of the girls from the brothel were leaning against the railings, smoking joints. They regarded Isabella coolly as she paused to check the address.

"What are you looking for?" one of the women asked.

"The tattoo parlour," she replied in her serviceable Arabic. "Do you know where it is?"

"Round the back."

"Thank you."

There was an alleyway that led around to the rear of the grocery store. There was a neat and tidy courtyard and, facing onto it, a door that had been painted in a multitude of different colours. The sign above the door read "Johnny's Ink," and when she opened it, a bell tinkled musically. She went inside. The parlour was small and colourful, with hand-drawn flashes that advertised the tattoos framed and hung on the walls. The floor was tiled in white and black chequerboard and a large canvas had been painted with the parlour's logo: a *femme fatale* in a tight dress, smoking a cigarette in a holder as a devil in a top hat inked a tattoo on her arm.

There was no one there.

"Hello?" she called out.

A man's voice came from a second room: "Hold on."

There was a pause, and then Metallica's "Master of Puppets" played out, loud, from speakers hung from the walls.

The man who came out of the room was tall and muscular. He looked like a soldier. His hair was shaved short, and every inch of exposed skin was covered in tattoos.

"Hello," he said with a wide smile. "How can I help you?"

"Are you Johnny?"

"I sure am." He had a lazy American drawl. "And who are you?"

"Isabella Rose. My mother used to come here."

His eyes went wide. "Oh shit," he said, and then, "I'm sorry . . . my language."

"Don't worry," she said, her turn to smile.

"No, I . . . I . . ." he frowned, floundering.

"You like Metallica?" she said, nodding up at the speakers.

"I do. You too . . . I mean, if you want, I could . . ."

"I love them," she said. "You got 'Ride the Lightning'?"

He looked relieved. "Sure I do. Hold on."

He went back into the other room, and after a short moment, "Fight Fire with Fire" started to play.

He came through to the reception again.

"There," he said. He smiled awkwardly again. "Your mother liked them, too."

"Yes. She did."

"How is she?" He said it diffidently, as if he already knew the answer, but the question still had to be asked.

"She's not here anymore."

"Oh shit . . . I'm sorry."

"Thank you."

"I knew she was ill," he said.

"Cancer."

"Yeah, that's right. Cancer. When did she pass?"

"Four months ago."

"Oh, man. I'm really, *really* sorry."

She nodded.

He forced a hesitant smile and changed the subject. "So what can I do for you?"

"I want a tattoo."

He looked at her with dubious regard. "What's your name, sweetheart?"

"Isabella."

"And how old are you?"

"Sixteen."

"Really?"

She nodded.

"I'm going to need to see something that says that. If I tattoo someone younger than that, I could end up losing my license."

She reached into her bag and took out the fake passport. "Here," she said.

Johnny looked at her picture and the details alongside it, his dubious expression slowly changing into one of mild surprise. "Yep, there we go. Sixteen. Nearly seventeen. Sorry about that. You look younger."

"It's alright. I get it a lot."

He stepped aside and pointed to the other room. "You go on through there, take your sweater off and make yourself comfortable. You want a soft drink?"

"Do you have any Coke?"

"Sure. Go on, go through. I'll be there in a minute."

The second room had a couch, a wheeled stool, more art on the walls and a fridge with beers inside it. Isabella took off her light cardigan and hung it up on a hook fixed to the wall. She was wearing a singlet underneath so that her arms and shoulders were bare. She knew what to expect. She sat down on the couch.

Her mother had sat here, too. On the same couch.

Four times.

Four different tattoos.

There had been no time for the fifth.

Isabella had forced herself to be strong, like her mother had been, but there were times, like now, when it was still raw, like the stitching on a wound had been picked open, exposing the hurt inside. She gasped a little, her eyes prickling with tears, but she breathed deeper and wiped the tears away, and in a moment, she had it all back under control again. She would be strong.

"Here," Johnny said, returning with a cold bottle of Coke.

He gave the bottle to her, took a bottle of beer from the fridge, popped the top and touched the neck against hers. He took a long sip and set it down on the table next to his magnums.

"You got an idea what you want?"

"A rose. Like my mother's."

"Funny you should say that. I was looking back at the designs I did for her just last week. Hold on." He shuffled through a sheaf of transfers on the table and picked one out. "Here. We were always going to finish the sleeve off. She had two more to do, five and six."

He handed it to her. Of course, she remembered the four roses that her mother had worn on her arm, running all the way down from her shoulder. The completed sleeve would have been beautiful.

The roses were gorgeous, deep blood-red petals, long and sinuous stems and vivid green leaves. They would have matched the others on her arm.

"What do you think?"

"Very pretty."

Johnny smiled at her praise.

"The fifth and the sixth roses. The ones she didn't have. Can you do those for me?"

"Sure. Would be good for me, too. I hate not finishing a design after I've drawn it. You know she was having these roses done one at a time? She said she was ticking things off a list, adding one whenever she'd done whatever it was she was doing."

"That's exactly what she was doing."

"She never did tell me what was on that list. Did she tick the last things off?"

"Yes," Isabella said. "She did."

"That's good. Nothing as bad as a job that's only halfway done." He took the design from her, sat on the wheeled stool and kicked back to the table. He picked up the transfer and rolled back to her again. He cleaned her skin, took a stick deodorant, daubed it over the long space between her shoulder and elbow and then rested the transfer there.

"Last chance," he said. "You still sure you want to do this?"

"Yes."

"I ain't gonna lie, sweetheart. It's going to hurt some."

"That's alright," she said. "I don't mind a little pain."

⌣   ⌣

Isabella wandered through the square. It was big and mad, and it had frightened her when she had first arrived with her mother last year, but as the weeks had passed, she had grown to love the crazy rush of it, the hordes of people, the haggling, the clamour. The change from day to night was best of all. The fires were lit, the lights started to glow against the gloaming, the smells became richer and more appetising. The muezzin's call rang out from the minarets of the mosque, and overhead a flock of fat gulls circled the market, waiting to gorge on the abundant scraps.

The last four months had been a mad, dizzying blur. Michael Pope had driven her away from the hospital as the police and the black SUVs with tinted windows descended upon it. Her mother's plan for her had been to catch the train to Philadelphia and then fly out of the airport there, but he had suggested that would be too dangerous. She had been too frightened to demur. He had driven west to Charlotte, instead, and Douglas International. They had taken a domestic flight to Atlanta and then flown from there, direct to Paris. They transferred again and flew Air Maroc to Marrakech.

Isabella had slept on the flights. She had been smothered by the urge to sleep, and since she felt a little uncomfortable talking to Pope, she had surrendered to it. When she did awake, she would look at him through the slits of her half-closed eyes. As they transited through Charlotte and Atlanta, she noticed that he was watchful and alert. He looked very able, and Isabella felt safe with him.

They had arrived in Paris. Pope had been uncomfortable when she had thanked him for his help and told him that she would be fine. He was reluctant to let her leave, but really, what could he have done? Her passport might have been fake but it was a *good* fake, and it recorded that she was sixteen years old, almost an adult, and he was no relation to her. There was also the problem that he clearly had no idea what he should do with her. He couldn't take her back to England with him, especially if she didn't want to go.

And if she *had* gone with him, what would he do with her next? Foster parents again? Isabella would never have accepted that, and Pope had known it.

Instead, he had written his telephone number on the back of a magazine and told her that if she ever needed him, then all she had to do was call. She had torn the page out, folded it and slipped it into her pocket, although she had no intention of ever using it.

Pope had told her one more thing. He had seen her mother when they were in London, and Beatrix had asked him to wipe every trace of her daughter from the record. He said that he had done that. As far as the rest of the world was concerned, Isabella Rose did not exist.

And then that was that. His flight home left before hers, and so he had hugged her, wished her good luck, and left her alone with the swell of travellers in the departures lounge.

She had her mother's credit card, and it had been a simple enough thing to purchase an onward ticket to Marrakech. Her hopes had originally been pinned on Mohammed and Fatima. That had been the plan. Her mother had said that they would be responsible for her in her absence, and yet there was no sign of them. The telephone number that she had called from the airport went unanswered. Her mother had given her the name and address of a café in Marrakech that she was to visit in the event that she couldn't reach Mohammed, but the proprietor said that he hadn't seen him or his wife for several days. She had visited every day for the first month, but there was no sign of them. Then, at the start of the second month, the proprietor told her that he had heard Mohammed and Fatima had been seen with a group of four white men, just after the attack on the riad. They had been forced into the back of a car and driven away.

Isabella knew what that meant.

Alone, then. She would do it alone.

She kept walking.

She had something else she needed to do.

———

Isabella had found an envelope in her mother's bag before she dropped it in the trash at the Chesapeake hotel. The envelope had been addressed to her. Inside, there was a small key and a piece of paper with an address written on it. She had visited the address during her first week back in Marrakech. It was a garage, similar to the one where they had kept their Jeep, a single door in a terrace of identical lock-ups in a run-down part of town. She had stepped up to the metal door and inserted her key, but she hadn't been able to turn it.

It was too soon.

It was still too raw.

And she didn't know what she might find.

Today, though, with the fresh tattoo burning on her shoulder, it felt like the right time.

The garage was a good distance from the centre of town, but she decided to walk. Exercise always helped her to think, and she wanted to prepare herself for what she might find.

She reached the garages, and, by dint of her mother's repeated exhortations, waited at the end of the road for twenty minutes and observed the comings and goings. She had no reason to suspect that there was anything to be fearful of now that Control was dead, but, from what she understood, her mother had landed a hefty blow to the financial interests of the company that he had worked for. She had set up a Google Alert for "Manage Risk" and had read a stream of articles that described how its stock price had plummeted in just a month. Contracts had been lost and important clients were shunning the business. Isabella wasn't particularly concerned that they would come after her since it would do them no good, but it still paid to be watchful.

She wore the key on a piece of string around her neck, next to the key for the front door. She reached down to her chest, her fingers closing around the metal that had warmed against her hot skin, and withdrew it. She checked back up and down the street again, satisfied herself that nothing was amiss and pushed the key into the rusting lock. It was stiff, and she had to twist it hard, but it turned, and she heaved the door up halfway.

She crouched down and slipped beneath it.

It was impossible to see anything inside. There were no windows or roof lights, and the dim lamp light that leaked in from beneath the door was devoured quickly by the darkness. She took out her cellphone, switched on the flashlight app and shone the beam around the interior.

The wall Isabella was facing had been equipped with metal cupboards and racking. She played the beam onto the racking and saw an arsenal of weapons: semi-automatic pistols, rifles, submachine guns, shotguns. She placed her phone on the table, the flashlight pointing up, reached up to the rack and took down an AR-15 semi-automatic with a thirty-round magazine. She pushed the stock against her shoulder, balancing its weight between her hands.

It felt good.

She opened the cupboards and shone her torch into them. She saw boxes upon boxes of ammunition, knives, grenades and other combat equipment.

Her mother had said once that there was a backup weapons cache should the riad ever be compromised.

Here it was.

Isabella swung the light around one final time, and just as she was about to leave, she saw the envelope that had been taped to one of the cupboard doors. She tore it free and stuffed it into her pocket.

She ducked down beneath the door, closed it after her and made doubly sure that it was locked.

Then, tired, she headed for home.

———⌣———

Isabella walked to the new riad. It was on the Rue Kaa El Machraa, on the other side of town from the place that she had shared with her mother. It was approached through the same warren of alleyways and passages, ever-narrowing, dark and mysterious. She turned right and then left, stepped over two of the local boys flicking marbles in the light of a kerosene lamp, and finally reached the thick oak door that reminded her of before. The small sign fixed on the wall next to it announced the "Riad Farnatchi."

Her own place.

Purchased with her own money.

She took the key from the chain she wore around her neck and unlocked the door. She stepped inside, dropped her bag on the table in the vestibule, shut the door and locked it behind her. Security was important. This was Marrakech, after all, and caution was a characteristic of her mother that had proven to be particularly infectious. She never took her safety for granted.

She collected her bag again, stepped out of the covered vestibule and into the open courtyard. This riad was smaller than the old place and much less opulent, with plenty of work still to do to fix the crumbling walls and the dated décor, but Isabella didn't mind any of that. It was her own place. Her little sanctuary. And she liked the idea of a project.

Renewal.

That seemed appropriate.

The firm of local builders that she had hired for the renovation had finished for the day. Their haphazard scaffolding was erected along the wall that was in the worst condition, the one that had almost completely collapsed. Their tools and buckets were lined up on the platform. It looked like they had made good progress today, the fresh course of bricks reaching up almost to the first floor.

The men were good at their job, but they were not above trying to take advantage of a young client whom they must have seen as ripe for exploitation. Their early work had been substandard, but they had tried to persuade her that it was acceptable. They had stopped doing that when Isabella immediately cut off their funding. She had insisted on payment on completion of the job and would not be moved from that position. The men learned quickly that she could be stubborn, and eventually she had bent them to her will. It was a question of setting expectations. They had to be taught.

Isabella knew what she wanted. She had a very clear vision in her mind's eye. She would turn the airy, light-filled space into somewhere that could be her own private sanctuary. She had chosen a soothing, elephant-grey palette that she would brighten with careful splashes of colour, like the deep-pile scarlet Beni Ouarain carpet on the balcony outside her bedroom on the first floor that she had bought from a Berber market in the mountains. The décor would be a pastiche of Moroccan and European vintage finds, with tribal textiles and quirky objets d'art. The plunge pool was to be tiled in emerald and surrounded by lime-green easy chairs. Her most recent purchase had been a Berber tent which she had arranged on the roof, and she liked to sit up there beneath the canvas and watch the sun sink down into the desert.

None of this had been cheap, but money had not been a concern for her. Beatrix had left her very well provided for indeed. Most importantly, she had established an account in Isabella's name at a branch of the First Caribbean International Bank. Isabella had used her credit card to pay for a week in Marrakech's best hotel as soon as she had arrived, using the time to gather herself, and then she had purchased a return flight to George Town in the Cayman Islands to visit the bank. The manager said that he was expecting her, and once the administrative necessities required to identify her had been taken care of, he had given her unrestricted access to the account.

One and a quarter million pounds.

Her mother had been right: it was more than she would ever need.

Two hundred thousand purchased the dilapidated riad, and another one hundred thousand would restore it.

She went up to the roof, lit the lanterns that she had placed around the wide space and sat down beneath the canvas awning. The top of her arm was swathed in a clear dressing, and she pulled her sleeve up to her shoulder to let it breathe. The design of the flowers was still visible beneath the slathering of Lubriderm. Johnny had done an excellent job. The two roses were just like her mother's.

The design had been completed.

That was exactly what she wanted.

A dusty sirocco blew across the rooftops and rustled the canvas. The flames jerked in the breeze. The call to prayer sounded, a rasping voice thrown far and wide by squawking speakers. Isabella watched and listened, absorbing the rhythm of the city. She touched the tattoo with her fingertips, little thorns of irritation prickling her flesh.

She had done what her mother had always asked of her. Beatrix had tried to recant a year's worth of instructions on the night before she left for her rendezvous at the drive-in, but Isabella had ignored her. It had been her mother's illness talking. She knew that she didn't mean it. *Couldn't* have meant it. She had been sure about that. Her mother's work had driven her.

It needed to be finished.

It *had* to be finished.

And now it was.

She blinked back more tears. Her childhood had bred in her an instinctive fear of stability. It had taught her not to get comfortable, that nothing was forever. There had been foster parents whom she had grown to like, some she had even loved. Other homes had been unpleasant, full of cruelty and unkindness. It had been easier to treat them all the same, remember that they were all transient, good and bad, and that something else would replace them in due time. Because it always did. Her mother had explained why that was: Control did not want her to stay in one place for too long because it would make her easier to find.

Even the year that she had spent with her mother had been the same, in the end.

Everything came to an end.

She looked out at the great expanse of the city, the myriad lights that prickled the dark, the throng of people in the streets and, above it all, the climbing saucer of the moon.

Would this come to an end, too?

She took the envelope from her pocket and stared at it for a full fifteen minutes. She ran her finger along the long edge, felt the prick of the four sharp corners. Then, before she could change her mind, she slipped her finger inside the flap and sliced it open.

There was a note in her mother's neat script.

Be prepared. XXX.

She stood and moved to the balustrade, rested her hands on the cooling stone and looked out over the city.

Her city.

Would this come to an end?

Maybe it would.

Maybe someone would come for her, after all.

But if it did end, if they did come, she would make sure of one thing.

She would respect her mother's final injunction.

And she would be ready.

Acknowledgements

I am indebted to the following for their help, all above and beyond the call of duty: Lucy Dawson (for her early edits and direction), Martha Hayes (for masterful and thoughtful editing), Detective Lieutenant (Ret'd) Edward L. Dvorak, Los Angeles County Sheriff's Department, and Joe D. Gillespie (for their advice on weapons and military matters), and Martin Fricke, U.S. Intelligence Community contractor (ret.).

The following members of Team Milton were also invaluable: Lee Robertson, Nigel Foster, Frank Wells. Gary Pugsley, Brian Ellis, Bob, Mel Murray, Phil Powell, Charlie, Matt Ballard, Edward Short, Desiree Brown, Don Lehman, Barry Franklin, Corne van der Merwe, Dawn Taybron, Paul Quish, Carl Hinds, Chuck Harkins, Don, Bernard Carlington, Julian Annells, Charles Rolfe, Michael Conway, Grant Brown, Rick Lowe, Randall Masteller, Steve Devoir, Chris Orrick, Mike Stephens, Rick Seymour, Pat Kirk, Dale McDonald, Robert Lass, Bill Dawson, Rob Carr, Ian Clarke, Chris Goodson, Jared Gerstein, Roman Pyndiura, Cecelia Blewett, David Schensted, Caleb Burton, Louis Pascolini, Sonny de Castro, John Hall, Matt Bawden, JKP, Richard Stewart, Bev Birkin, Dave Zucker, Steve Carter, Christian Bunyan, Daniel Caupel, Debra

Koltveit, George Wood, Linda French, Mark Garner, Phillip Silcox, John Olsakovsky, Melinda Doup, Janet Homes, Lynn Edey, Tim Adams, Steve Hancox, Martin Wynkoop, Kent, Mark Dibble, Jack Ott, William Longau, Dale Viljoen, James Frederick, David, Alan and Daniel Ostendorff.

About the Author

Photo © 2014 Tom Nicholson

Mark Dawson has worked as a lawyer and in the London film industry.

He has written three series: John Milton features a disgruntled government hit man trying to right wrongs in order to make amends for the things he's done; Beatrix Rose traces the headlong fight for justice of a wronged mother and trained assassin; and Soho Noir is set in the West End of London between 1940 and 1970. Mark lives in Wiltshire, in the UK, with his family.

You can find him at www.markjdawson.com, www.facebook.com/markdawsonauthor and on Twitter at @pbackwriter.

Printed in Great Britain
by Amazon